Chess for Children

Murray Chandler
Helen Milligan

Illustrations by Cindy McCluskey

GAMBIT

First published in the UK by Gambit Publications Ltd 2004
Reprinted 2006, 2007, 2008, 2009, 2010, 2011, 2012, 2013, 2014

ISBN-13: 978-1-904600-06-0
ISBN-10: 1-904600-06-9

DISTRIBUTION:
Worldwide (except USA): Central Books Ltd, 99 Wallis Rd, London E9 5LN, England.
Tel +44 (0)20 8986 4854 Fax +44 (0)20 8533 5821. E-mail: orders@Centralbooks.com

Gambit Publications Ltd, 99 Wallis Rd, London E9 5LN, England.
E-mail: info@gambitbooks.com
Website (regularly updated): www.gambitbooks.com

Edited by Bad Bishop Ltd
Typeset by Berfort Reproductions Ltd
Illustrations by Cindy McCluskey of FatKat Animation
Printed in the USA by Bang Printing, Brainerd, Minnesota

10

Gambit Publications Ltd
Directors: Dr John Nunn GM, Murray Chandler GM and Graham Burgess FM
German Editor: Petra Nunn WFM

Acknowledgements: Junior chess coaches Jonathan Tuck and Heather Lang for helpful suggestions; Eddie Sturgeon for typography; the Collister family, Christina Harvey, John & Chris Constable, Karen Chandler, Graham Burgess, John Nunn and Beverley Brackett for additional assistance.

CONTENTS

Introduction

Chess is the most exciting and challenging game of strategy ever invented. It has captivated enthusiasts for thousands of years, all around the world.

In a game of chess it is pure skill – not luck – that decides who wins. You and your opponent each start with 16 chessmen, on a chessboard of 64 squares. What happens next depends entirely on you. You use your forces to try and outwit your opponent, with the plan of checkmating his king. You might come up with a grand scheme to capture some enemy pieces. But a clever opponent might stop your plan, whilst hatching a devious scheme of his own! You'll need all of your powers of mental concentration to outplay someone at chess.

Learning to play chess is surprisingly easy. This book shows how all of the pieces move, and teaches chess notation plus some basic strategy. Soon you can enjoy playing games with your friends, or with any Grand Alligators of chess that might be passing.

PART ONE

★ **The Chessboard & Pieces** ★ **The Starting Position** ★ **How the Pieces Move** ★

It was raining, and George was bored with watching TV.

"I know what to do," said Kirsty, his pet alligator.

"Let's play chess. It's really easy. I'll teach you."

"That's a great idea," said George. "But I want to learn chess properly. So NO TALL TALES, or I'll flush you down the you-know-what."

"Me tell tales? No way!" said Kirsty.
"Did you know my Uncle was a Grandmaster?"

The Names of the Chess Pieces

Each player (whether playing with the white pieces or the black pieces) starts the game with 16 pieces. You have 8 pawns, 2 rooks, 2 knights, 2 bishops, 1 king and 1 queen. Here are symbols we use to show each piece:

♙ The white pawn   ♟ The black pawn

♘ The white knight   ♞ The black knight

♗ The white bishop   ♝ The black bishop

♖ The white rook   ♜ The black rook

♕ The white queen   ♛ The black queen

♔ The white king   ♚ The black king

All the pieces have their own special ways of moving, and capturing other pieces. We will look at their powers shortly.

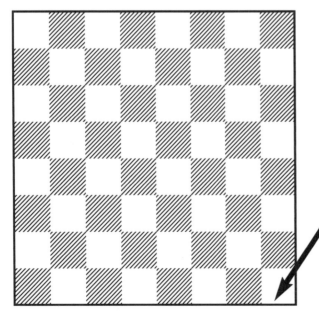

The Chessboard

Chess is played on an 8 x 8 board. When you play chess, be sure to place the chessboard correctly in front of you – with a *light square on your right-hand side.*

'**White on the right**' is the easy way to remember. Perhaps some great chess historian could explain why, but for the moment, that is just the way it is!

The Starting Position

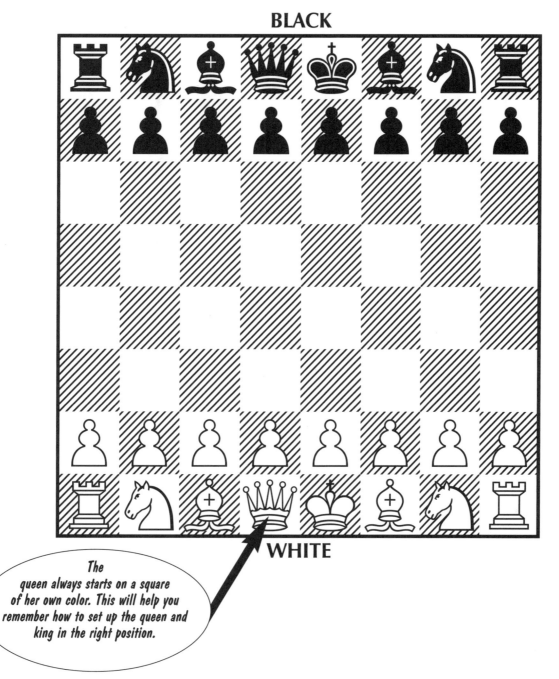

BLACK

WHITE

The queen always starts on a square of her own color. This will help you remember how to set up the queen and king in the right position.

Here are all the pieces and pawns set up in the starting position. Every game of chess begins from this position, with the pieces on these squares. The white pieces are at one end, and the black pieces are at the other.

Each player takes turns to make one move at a time. White always makes the first move, and Black replies with his move.

You win at chess if you **trap the enemy king**. When the enemy king is attacked, and has no escape, this is called "Checkmate!"

Win 1 point for every correct answer. These puzzles will test your skills at naming the pieces and setting up a chessboard correctly. *Write down* your answers if possible. *Solutions: page 108.*

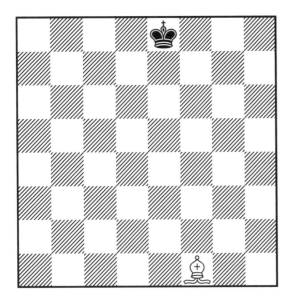

1) Name the chess pieces

There is one white piece and one black piece on this chessboard. Can you name which pieces they are?

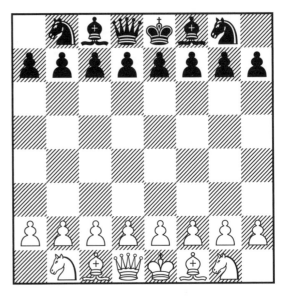

2) Spot the missing pieces

The players are ready to start a game – but there are four pieces missing! Can you work out which pieces are missing?

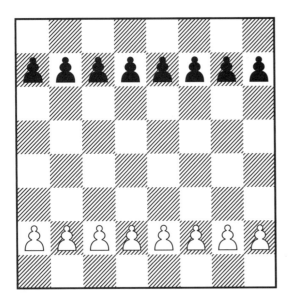

3) Count the pawns

The pawns are all in their starting positions. How many pawns are on the board at the start of a game of chess?

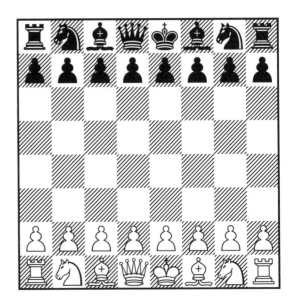

4) Count the knights

All the pieces are in their starting positions. How many knights are there on a chessboard at the start of a game?

How Bishops & Rooks Move

"This one is the bishop," said Kirsty.
"They move and capture only along the diagonals."

"That's not too hard," said George. "Bishop takes mouse!"

"That's nothing," said Kirsty. "I captured a moose once, at the old Lone Pine tournament of '79."

How the Bishop Moves ♗ ♝

Bishops move *diagonally*, in straight lines only. They can move as many squares as they like, right up to the edges of the board. They can move forward or backwards along the diagonals.

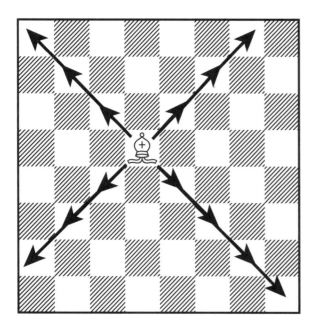

This white bishop can move to any of the squares shown by the arrows.

Bishops can't jump over pieces. The whole track that they run along must be clear of pieces or pawns. You can't go 'through' or jump over one of your own pieces or pawns. However, if one of your opponent's pieces or pawns stands in the way of your bishop, you can **capture it**, take it off the board, and put your bishop on its square.

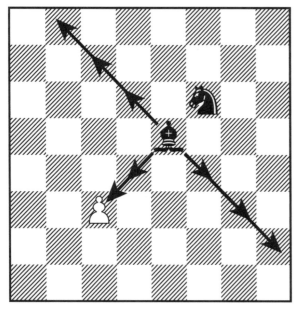

Here the black bishop can only move to the squares marked by the arrows.

The bishop *cannot* jump over pieces – you can see the black knight is blocking some of the bishop's possible moves.

However, the bishop *can* capture the white pawn if it wants.

How the Rook Moves ♖ ♜

You have two rooks. Sometimes you might hear people calling them 'castles', because that's what they look like, but real chess-players always call them rooks. Rooks move only in straight lines along the board. They can move forward or backwards (along the files) or side-to-side (along the ranks).

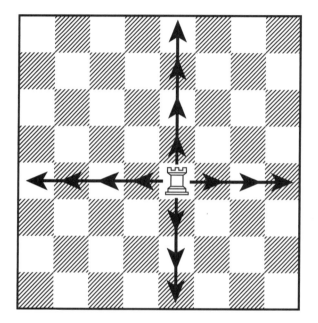

The white rook can move to any of the squares shown by the arrows.

Rooks capture exactly the same way that they move. They cannot jump over other pieces.

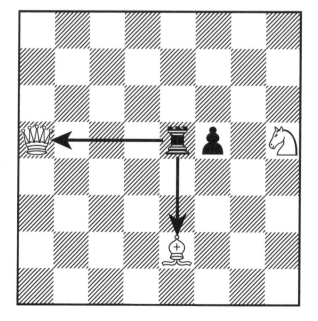

Here the black rook has a choice of two white pieces to capture. It can take the white bishop, or it can take the white queen.

But the black rook **cannot** take the white knight! The path is **blocked by his own pawn**.

Win 1 point for every correct answer. Bishops and rooks can move the length of the chessboard if they want, so think carefully about each puzzle. *Write down* your answers if possible. *Solutions: page 108.*

1) White to move
The white bishop can capture a black piece in this position. Is it the black knight or the black pawn?

2) Black to move
Can the black bishop capture the white queen in this position?

3) White to move
How many black pieces is the white rook attacking in this position?

4) Black to move
The black rook can capture just one white piece in this position. Which one?

How Queens & Kings Move

"The queen is a mighty piece, really powerful," said Kirsty. "It's like a bishop and rook combined."

"Wow," said George. "So the queen must be really valuable."

"It certainly is," said Kirsty. "When I captured Boris Spassky's queen and won the World Championships, Boris burst into tears."

"I hope Mom has cleaned the toilet," said George.

How the Queen Moves ♕ ♛

The queen can move along ranks and files (just like a rook). She can also move along diagonals (just like a bishop). She can move as many squares as she likes, right up to the edge of the board, in any direction.

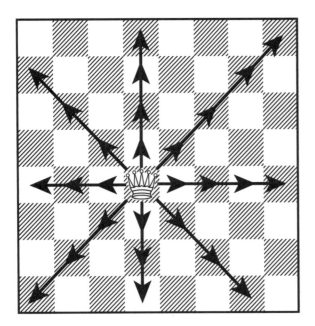

The queen can move as many squares as she likes, right up to the edge of the board.

But, just like bishops and rooks, the one thing a queen cannot do is jump over other pieces.

A queen can capture exactly the same way that she moves. But remember, the queen is a hugely powerful piece, and you will need to look after her carefully.

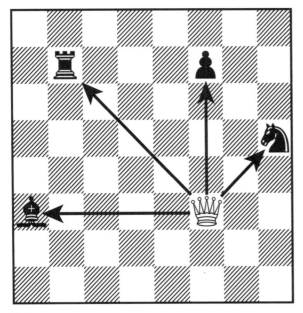

Here the mighty white queen is attacking four pieces at the same time. She can capture the black pawn, knight, rook or bishop.

However, capturing the black pawn here would be a terribly bad move. The black pawn is *protected* by the black rook. If the white queen took the black pawn, the black rook could capture the queen in reply!

How the King Moves ♔ ♚

The king can move one square in any direction: forward, backwards, left or right, or diagonally.

Here the black king can move to any of the eight squares shown by the arrows.

The king captures the same way as he moves. Here the white king could capture the black pawn, if he wanted.

The king seems like a weak piece – he can hardly move very far going just one square at a time. However, the king is actually *the most important piece on the board!*

Why is the king so important? Because the whole aim of a game of chess is to trap your opponent's king. If you can reach a position where you are threatening to take your opponent's king, and there is nothing he or she can do about it, then you have WON! It is called CHECKMATE and it ends the game!

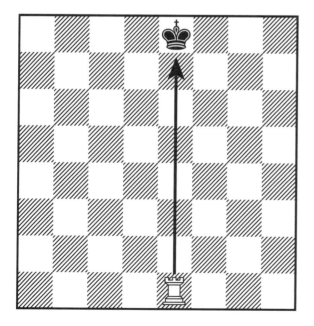

It is **check** when a king comes under attack. If your king is checked, you **must** get out of check immediately. You can never move your king into check either.

Here the black king is in **check**, because **he is attacked by the white rook**. Black **must** get out of check. In this position Black can get out of check by moving his king.

Win 1 point for every correct answer. These puzzles will test your king and queen moves. *Write down* your answers if possible. *Solutions: page 108.*

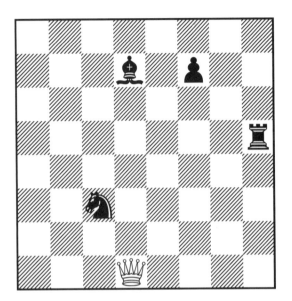

1) White to move
How many black pieces is the white queen attacking in this position?

2) Black to move
Can the black queen capture the white bishop in this position?

3) White to move
Can the white king capture any black pieces or pawns in this position?

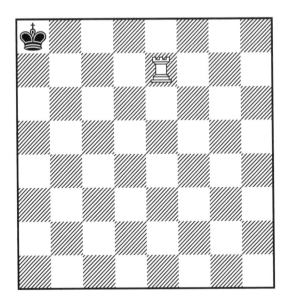

4) Black to move
How many legal moves does the black king have in this position? Remember, a king can never move into check!

How Pawns & Knights Move

"The knight is my favorite piece," said Kirsty. "It leaps over other pieces and moves in a tricky L-shape."

"Does it capture the same way?" asked George.
"It certainly does," said Kirsty. "You can attack lots of enemy pieces at the same time. In fact, that's exactly how I once beat a young Bobby Fischer in the Manhattan Junior Championships."

How the Pawns Move ♙ ♟

You have 8 pawns. They start the game in front of your pieces, and can only move forward. **Pawns never move backwards**.

Pawns can generally only move forward one square at a time. However, on their *very first move* they are allowed to move either one or two squares forward.

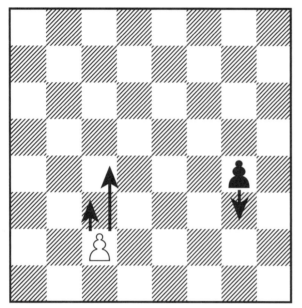

The black pawn (advancing *down* the board) has already moved. Therefore it can only move one square at a time from now on.

The white pawn is in its *starting position*, ready to advance *up* the board. Because it hasn't moved yet during the game, it can move either one or two squares forward.

Pawns cannot advance if the square ahead is blocked by another piece (either a piece of your own or your opponent's). But pawns *can* capture enemy pieces *diagonally*.

Pawns Capture *Diagonally*

Although pawns move by advancing straight ahead, when they *capture* they move differently. Pawns can capture enemy pieces that are one square ahead *diagonally*.

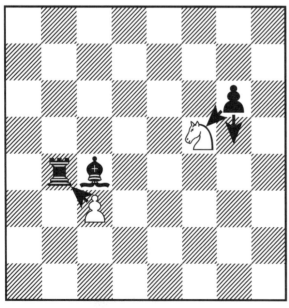

Here the black pawn can capture the white knight, OR it can move straight ahead.

Here the white pawn can capture the black rook. The white pawn **cannot** move straight ahead, as the black bishop is already there.

How the Knight Moves ♘♞

The knight hops in an L-shape, in any direction – forward, sideways or backwards. And it is the only piece that can jump over other pieces.

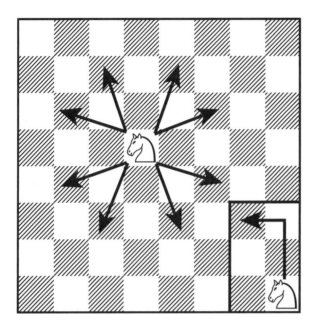

A knight in the center of the board has the choice of moving to any of eight different squares.

Here the arrow shows how the knight hops in an L-shape. To work out where your knight can go, think "**two-one.**" Move the knight **two squares** in one direction, and then **one square** sideways.

The knight captures exactly the same way as it moves. Take a look at the diagram below, and see which black pieces the white knight can choose to capture.

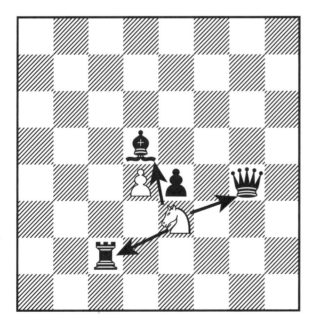

White to play

The white knight can capture any one of *three* black pieces! The black rook, queen and bishop are all under attack.

Note how the knight can even jump over the pawns to take the black bishop.

Did you know...
When a knight moves it always ends up on a square of the *opposite* color.

Win 1 point for every correct answer. Have you mastered those tricky pawn and knight moves? *Write down* your answers if possible. *Solutions: page 108.*

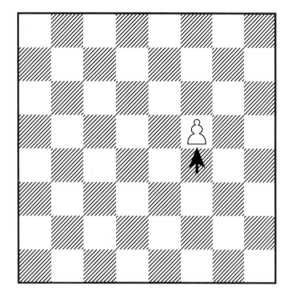

1) White to move
Here White moved his pawn one square forward (as shown by the arrow). Could the pawn have advanced two squares instead?

2) Black to move
Which white piece can the black pawn capture here? Is it the white bishop or the white rook?

3) White to move
The white knight can capture a black piece in this position. Is the knight attacking the black rook or the queen?

4) Black to move
The black knight has a choice of captures here. Exactly *how many* white pieces is the black knight attacking?

EXERCISES

Here are some fun training exercises. You'll need to get your chess set and board out, and do the exercises on that. Only move the white pieces. Perhaps later on you could ask Mom or Dad to test you on these exercises.

Exercise 1
CORNER TO CORNER

This tests your skill at making long bishop moves!

See if you can move your bishop all the way down the diagonal to the other corner (marked "X") in one go.

Exercise 2
ROMPING ROOK

Keep moving your rook until you reach the square marked X, and capture two black pawns on the way!

This means you need to move your rook four squares forward, then six squares sideways, and then three squares backwards.

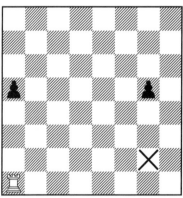

Exercise 3
HUNGRY HORSE

Keep moving your knight until you have captured both black pawns. Can you do it?

For perfect play do it in just six moves!

Exercise 4
HORRENDOUSLY HUNGRY HORSE

Make moves with the white knight to capture all eight black pawns.

Can you do it taking less than 3 minutes? If so you might soon be Grand Alligator standard!

MINI-CHESS GAMES

Well done for learning the basic chess moves! The next step is chess notation (page 24), but if you are really keen to start playing some chess straight away, you could try out these mini-chess training games. You'll need to have a parent, friend (or pet alligator) as your opponent.

These mini-chess games use just some of the pieces, for practice. White moves first, then Black, and you continue taking turns.

Did you know there is a "touch move" rule in chess? When you are playing a game, you can't change your mind and take moves back! If you touch a piece, you should move it.

Mini-Chess 1
THE PAWN GAME
White moves first, then take turns.

The first player to get a pawn right to the other end of the board will win!

Try to advance your pawns. Remember, the white pawns move up the board, and the black pawns move down the board.

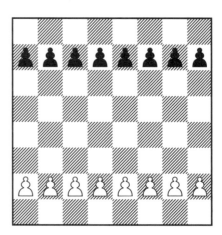

Mini-Chess 2
THE KNIGHT GAME
White moves first, then take turns.

The first player to capture all the enemy pawns will win!

Use your knights aggressively – they can leap out quickly to attack the enemy pawns.

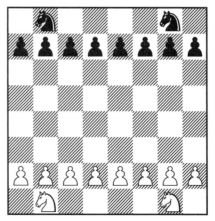

Mini-Chess 3
THE ROOK AND BISHOP GAME
White moves first, then take turns.

The first player to capture an enemy rook or bishop will win!

Did you remember to play the "touch move" rule? One trick is to sit on your hands until you have worked out which move to play!

PART TWO

★ **Learning Chess Notation** ★ **The Values of the Pieces** ★ **Practicing Moves** ★

Learning chess notation is easy. It enables you to play over chess games from books, and to write your moves down.
With practice you might even be able to play "blindfold chess" — calling your moves out without looking at the chessboard!

Learning Chess Notation

Now for something that will really impress your family and friends – reading and writing **algebraic chess notation!**

Here is an empty chessboard, with the algebraic notation coordinates written around the edges to help you.

You can see that the **files** – going **up** the board – are labeled **a, b, c, d, e, f, g, h**.

The **ranks** – going **across** the board – are labeled **1, 2, 3, 4, 5, 6, 7, 8** from White's side of the board.

The beauty of this grid-like system is that every square on the board has a name of its own, as you can see from this diagram.

Because **every square has its own name**, it is very easy to describe a move.

Let's work out which square the white king is standing on. You might already be able to work it out by yourself.

The arrows help to show that the king is standing on the **e-file**, and also on **rank number 4**.

Therefore, the king is standing on the square **e4**.

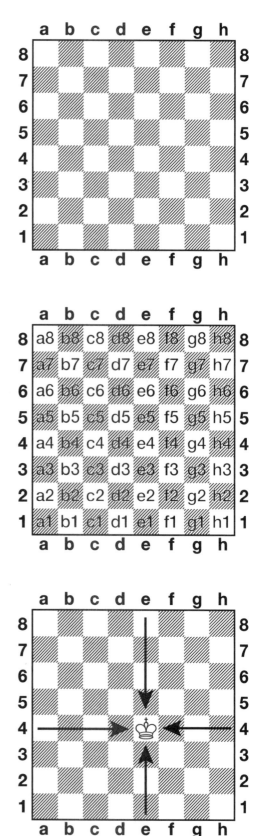

Practicing Chess Notation

Here are some pieces sitting on the chessboard. Work out the name of the square that each piece is on.

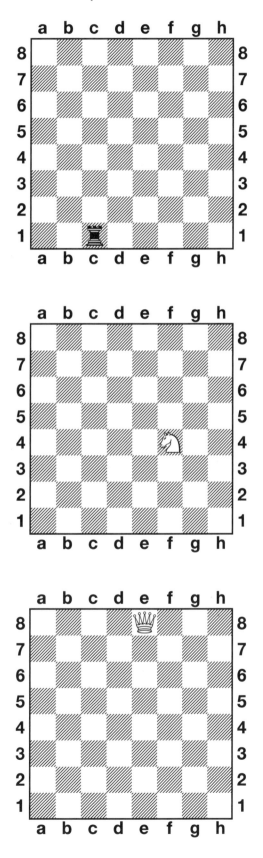

Where is the black rook?

The rook is on the c-file.
The rook is on rank number 1.
The rook is on **c1**.

Where is the white knight?

The knight is on the f-file.
The knight is on rank number 4.
The knight is on **f4**.

Where is the white queen?

The queen is on the e-file.
The queen is on rank number 8.
The queen is on **e8**.

How to Read & Write Chess Moves

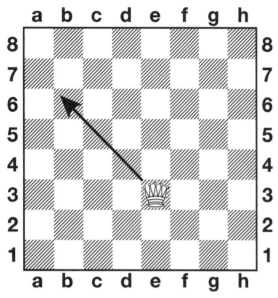

To record a chess move, you write down only the square it moves **to**. You also need to say which piece it is.

The move indicated by the arrow would be shown as: ♛**b6**.

This means the **queen** moves to the **b6 square**.

In chess books, you will usually see a little queen symbol, ♛. But when you're writing it down yourself, it is much easier to write the letter **Q** than to draw a queen.

Here are the letters we use for the pieces, to write the moves down ourselves.

N is for **Knight**   **Q** is for **Queen**
B is for **Bishop**   **K** is for **King**
R is for **Rook**

There is no symbol or letter needed to show pawn moves. We'll explain that in a moment.

You are probably wondering why we use the letter **N** for a **K**night! This is because **K** is kept for the **K**ing. Besides, 'knight' sounds like it begins with N.

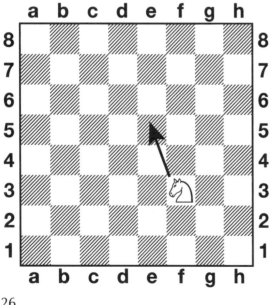

Let's practice writing down the move shown by the arrow in the diagram. White's **knight** is moving to the **e5** square (shown as ♘**e5** if we saw it in a book).

If you were writing the move yourself, it would be written:
Ne5

How to Read & Write Chess Moves

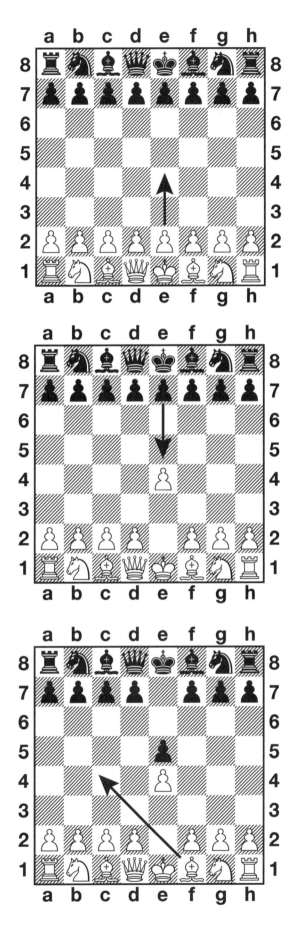

We don't use any symbols for pawns. You just give the destination square. Because of the way pawns move there is no confusion, as only one pawn can move to the square. It is also usual to number the moves. So we show the move indicated by the arrow as:

1 e4

This means on **move 1** of the game the white pawn moved to the **e4 square**. The next diagram shows the completed move.

Now it is Black's turn! Let's say Black replies to White's first move, by moving his own pawn to the e5 square. You write this next to the white move. So the recorded moves so far would now be written:

1 e4   e5

The next diagram shows the position.

Each side has played one move. Now, on move **two**, let's say White decides to move his **bishop** to the **c4 square**. After that move, the complete game notation so far would be written like this:

1 e4   e5
2 ♗c4

Some Facts About Algebraic Chess Notation

- Algebraic chess notation is used all over the world. You could even understand the moves of a chess game in a Russian magazine!

- A different chess notation, called Descriptive Notation, was popular some years ago. But these days most people use the simpler algebraic.

Event __USA Championship__ Date __2002__
White __A Shabalov__ Black __L Christiansen__
Opening _____ Opponent's Grade _____

#	White	Black		#	White	Black
1	d4	Nf6		26	Qd3	Nxg2
2	c4	e6		27	Kxg2	Qh4
3	Nf3	b6		28	Kg1	Nxf2
4	Nc3	Bb7		29	Qf1	Rxc1
5	a3	d5		30	Rxc1	Ne4
6	cxd5	exd5		31	Nxe4	dxe4
7	g3	Bd6		32	Qf2	Qh5
8	Bg2	0-0		33	f5	Kh7
9	0-0	Nbd7		34	Qf4	Rf6
10	Bf4	Bxf4		35	Rf1	Bh3
11	gxf4	c5		36	Rc1	Bxf5
12	e3	Rc8		37	Nxf5	Rxf5
13	Rc1	Ne4		38	0-1	
14	Ne2	Qe7		39		
15	Ng3	Rfd8		40		
16	Bh3	Rc7		41		
17	Qe2	Nf8		42		
18	Rfd1	Bc8		43		
19	Bg2	Bg4		44		
20	dxc5	bxc5		45		
21	Qc2	Rd6		46		
22	Re1	Ng6		47		
23	b4	h6		48		
24	Nd4	Nh4		49		
25	bxc5	Rxc5		50		

A typical scoresheet of a game might look like this. In serious competitions both players must write out a scoresheet during the game.

This game (from the USA Championship in Seattle) lasted 37 moves. Black won when White decided his position was lost, and RESIGNED.

Games between strong players often end with one player resigning. A player can resign at any time if he thinks his position is hopeless.

How to Read & Write Chess Moves

We've seen how easy it is to record the first few moves of a game in algebraic notation. Now let's see how you write down the capture symbol.

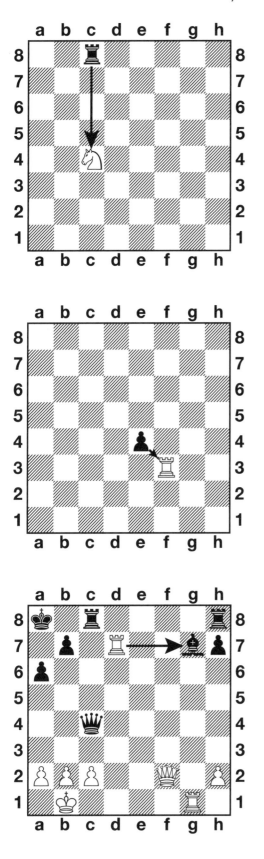

When a piece takes another piece, it is helpful to indicate this by writing the symbol "**x**" for capture. For example, in this position the black rook can capture the white knight. This is written:

1...♖xc4

You'll also notice there are three dots after the move number 1. This shows it is a move by Black.

In this position the black pawn can capture the white rook. We write this move as:

1...exf3

The black pawn came from the **e**-file and took the rook on **f3**.

Here's a tricky one – White can capture the black bishop with **either** of his two rooks. So writing 1 ♖**xg7** is not quite correct. We need to show *which* rook makes the capture!

1 ♖dxg7

The notation shows that it is the rook on the **d**-file that makes the capture. White's **rook** on the **d**-file captures the black bishop on **g7**.

Win 1 point for every correct answer. Your challenge here is to write down, in **algebraic chess notation**, the move shown by the arrow in each diagram. *Solutions: page 108.*

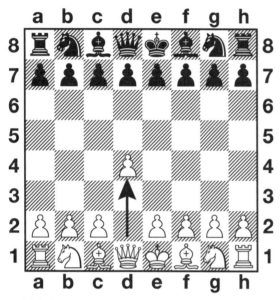

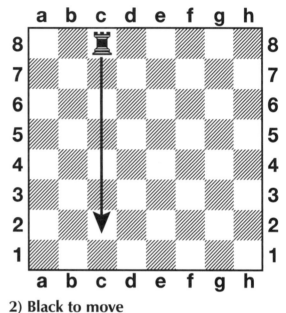

1) White to move
On his first move, White has advanced his d-pawn two squares, to the d4 square. How would you write this move in chess notation?

2) Black to move
How would you write the rook move (shown by the arrow) that Black is about to make?

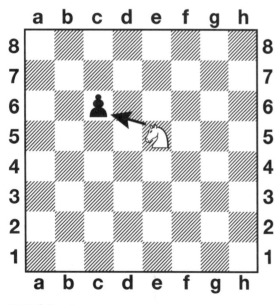

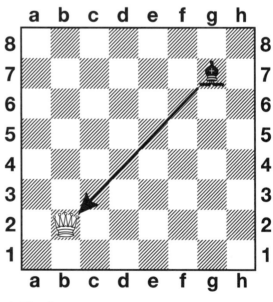

3) White to move
The white knight is about to capture the black pawn. How would you write this move down?

4) Black to move
The black bishop is about to capture the white queen. How would you write this move down?

The Values of the Pieces

When playing a game, try not to lose your valuable pieces!
A player who can capture enemy pieces for nothing is likely to win the game.

The Values of the Pieces

By now you will have noticed that the different chess pieces all have different ways of moving. Because some pieces move further and attack more swiftly than others, this makes them more powerful. So they are also more valuable.

This chart gives a useful guide to how much each piece is worth. It compares the pieces in value to a single pawn.

A KNIGHT = 3 pawns ♟ ♟ ♟

A BISHOP = 3 pawns ♟ ♟ ♟

A ROOK = 5 pawns ♟ ♟ ♟ ♟ ♟

A QUEEN = 9 pawns ♟ ♟ ♟ ♟ ♟ ♟ ♟ ♟ ♟

THE KING cannot be valued. He is too important!
If your king is trapped you lose the game. So you could say the king is worth **100 pawns,** or even more!

The Minor Pieces

You can see that the **knights** and the **bishops** (also known as **minor pieces**) are both considered to be worth about **three pawns** each. This is despite the fact that they move in completely different ways. The bishop is long-range, swooping down the diagonals. The knight, though short-range, has different talents. It is the only piece which can jump over other pieces, and its tricky "L" shaped move is great for double attacks!

The Major Pieces

You can see that the **rooks** (worth five pawns each) and the **queen** (worth nine pawns) are very valuable pieces. Rooks and queens are also known as the **major pieces**. They are extremely powerful, and can control many squares on the chessboard. For this reason, you have to take especially good care not to lose them by accident.

The Values of the Pieces

Now that you know the value of each piece, it is possible to work out if a swap of pieces might be good for you.

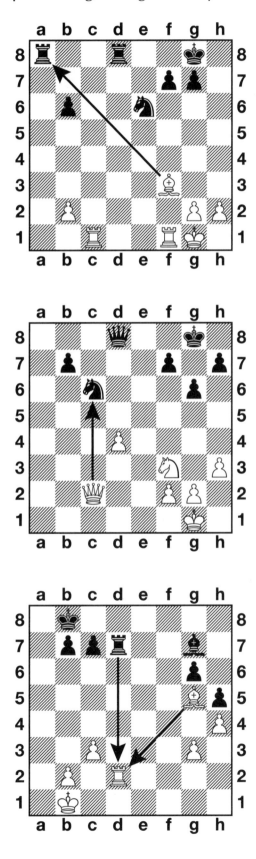

White to move
With the swap 1 ♗xa8 ♖xa8, White wins the black rook – but loses his own bishop in return.
A bishop is worth 3 pawns – but a rook is worth 5 pawns. So it was a good trade for White.

White to move
Should the white queen capture the black knight?

Absolutely NOT! After 1 ♕xc6 Black would reply 1...bxc6. White's valuable queen (worth nine pawns) would have been lost for a knight (worth only three pawns). A crazy swap like this would lose White the game for sure.

Black to move
1...♖xd2 2 ♗xd2 is an equal trade. Black gives up one of his valuable rooks, but in return has gained one of White's rooks.
The trade is equal in material terms – neither side has won or lost from the swap. Trading same-value pieces like this is routine.

Win 1 point for every correct answer. This test will show how well you have learnt the relative values of each piece. *Solutions: page 108.*

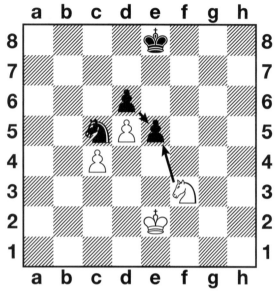

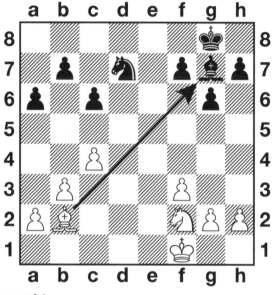

1) White to move

With 1 ♘xe5 dxe5 White captures a pawn but loses his knight. Is this is a good trade or a bad trade for White?

2) White to move

1 ♗xg7 ♚xg7 is a swap of the white bishop for the black bishop. Is this swap good, bad or equal?

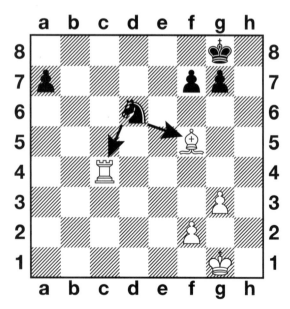

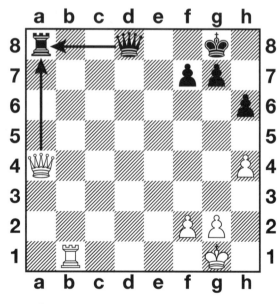

3) Black to move

Here there is a choice of undefended white pieces to capture. Should Black prefer to capture the white bishop or the white rook?

4) White to move

The white queen can exchange itself for the black rook with 1 ♕xa8 ♕xa8. Is swapping the queen for a rook a good idea for White?

Practicing Moves & Captures

A great way to improve is by playing lots of games against your friends.
Chess can be played anywhere and anytime.

Practicing Bishop Moves & Captures

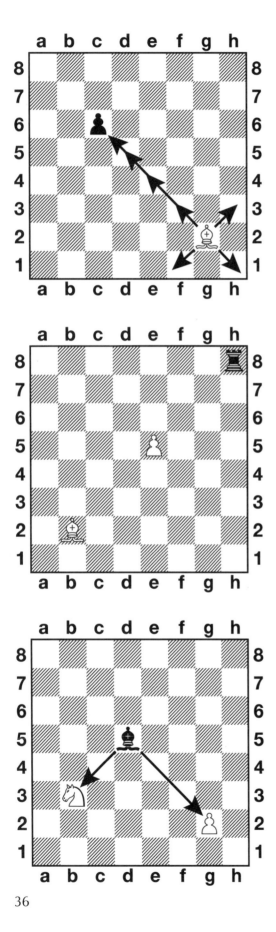

White to move

Bishops move along diagonals. Can you work out which squares the white bishop can move to? Well, they are f1, h1, h3, f3, e4 and d5.

The bishop can also **capture** the **black pawn on c6**. We write this as:
1 ♗xc6

White to move

The black rook is on the same diagonal as the white bishop. So can the bishop capture the rook?

No! White's own pawn on the e5 square is in the way. It blocks the attack. Bishops **cannot jump over pieces**, even those from your own side.

Black to move

Bishops are long-range pieces, and can easily attack along two diagonals simultaneously. Here the black bishop is attacking two white pieces.

The bishop can capture the white pawn:
1...♗xg2

or the bishop can capture the white knight:
1...♗xb3

Practicing Rook Moves & Captures

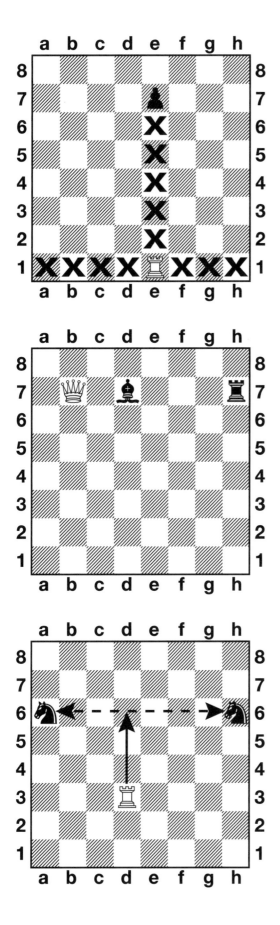

White to move

Rooks move along files and ranks. Like bishops, they are long-range pieces.

In this position the rook can go to all the squares marked.

The rook could also capture the black pawn:
1 ♖xe7

Black to move

Is the black rook attacking the white queen in this position?

No! The black bishop is in the way, and rooks cannot jump over pieces.

White to move

There is a good move in this position.

White can move his rook to attack both black knights at the same time. He plays:
1 ♖d6

Practicing Queen Moves & Captures

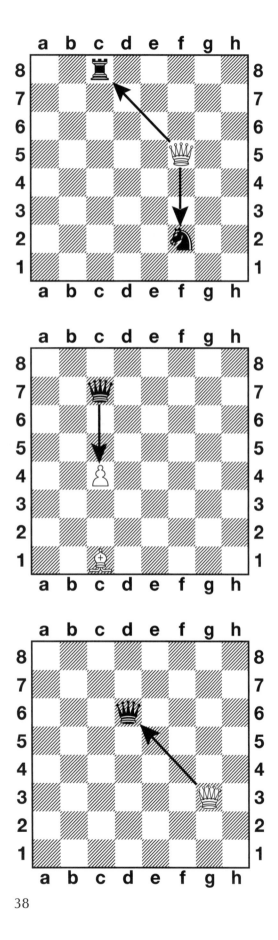

White to move

Remember, queens can move backwards as well as forward, and in straight lines and along diagonals.

Here the white queen could capture the black rook:
1 ♕xc8

Or, the queen could move backwards to capture the black knight:
1 ♕xf2

Black to move

Queens can't jump over other pieces! Here the black queen **can** capture the white pawn:
1...♕xc4

But the queen **cannot** instead capture the white bishop. The white pawn is currently in the way.

White to move

Here's a funny situation. The white queen and the black queen are both attacking each other! If it were Black's turn to move, he could capture the white queen.

Fortunately for White, it is his turn to move. With the move:
1 ♕xd6
White gets in first and wins the black queen.

Practicing King Moves & Captures

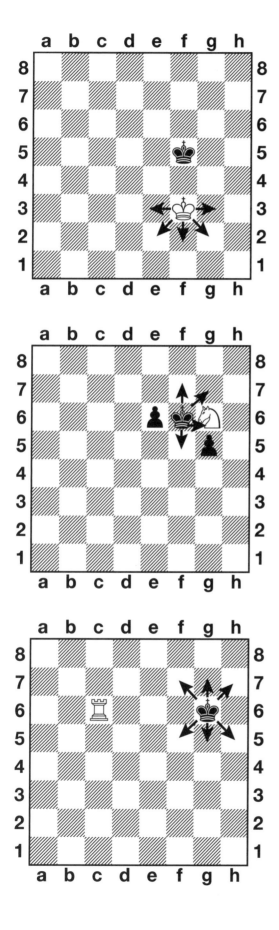

White to move

The white king is on the f3 square. It can move to e2, e3, f2, g2 and g3.

Here White **cannot** advance with 1 ♔e4, or 1 ♔f4, or 1 ♔g4. This is because the black king on f5 controls those squares.

Remember, two kings **can never move next to each other**. They would each be in check from the other king!

Black to move

The black king is on the f6 square. It can take the white knight, **1...♚xg6**. Or the king could move to three other squares: f7, g7 or f5.

The king cannot move to the e7 or e5 squares, as these are squares the white knight controls. You cannot move your king **into** check.

Black to move

Here the black king is under attack – **in check** – from the white rook. But it is not a big problem here, as there are six different moves possible to escape from the check.

The black king can move to f7, g7, h7, f5, g5, or h5.

Practicing Pawn Moves & Captures

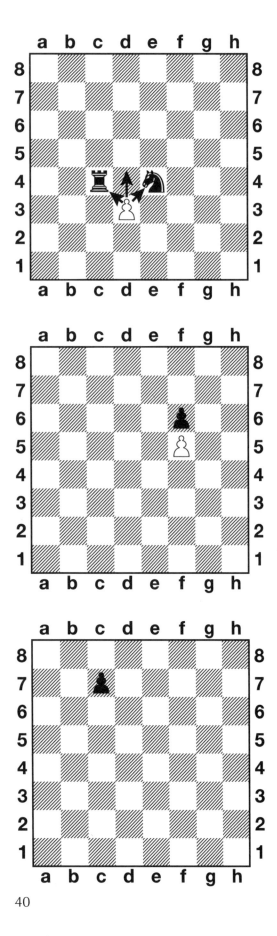

White to move

The white pawn (on the **d3** square) can choose between **three** different moves.

It can move straight forward one square:
1 d4

Or it can capture the black rook diagonally:
1 dxc4

Or it can capture the black knight diagonally!
1 dxe4

White to move

Which moves can the white pawn make? Here the white pawn – on the f5 square – is blocked by the black pawn. So the white pawn *cannot move forward.*

It cannot capture the black pawn, because pawns only capture diagonally. We also know that pawns cannot move backwards.

So the white pawn cannot move at all!

Black to move

Here's a tricky one. Which possible moves can the black pawn make? Normally a pawn just moves one square ahead, but here it is *still in the original starting position.*
So the black pawn has a choice.

It can move one square forward:
1...c6

Or it can move two squares forward:
1...c5

Practicing Knight Moves & Captures

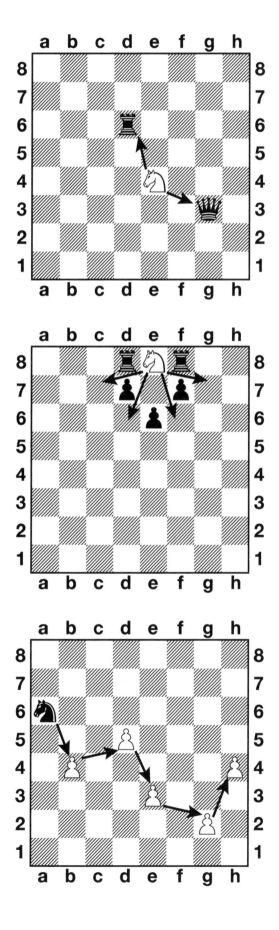

White to move

You'll remember that knights move in an unusual "L" shape. If one of your opponent's pieces or pawns is on a square your knight can move to, you might be able to capture it.

Here you can capture the black rook:
1 ♘xd6

Or you can capture black queen:
1 ♘xg3

White to move

Knights are special because they can jump over anything. Here the white knight is surrounded by black pieces, but can escape from trouble by jumping over them.

Here the knight can jump to the safe squares c7, d6, f6 or g7.

Black to move

Practice capturing with your knight in this mini "knight's tour" exercise. See if you can eat up all five white pawns, by making five moves in a row with your knight.

Of course, this would not happen in a real game. You can't make more than one move in a row – your opponent would protest!

Win 1 point for every correct answer. These exercises will test how well you can make basic chess moves and captures. If you can, write your answer in algebraic chess notation. *Solutions: page 108.*

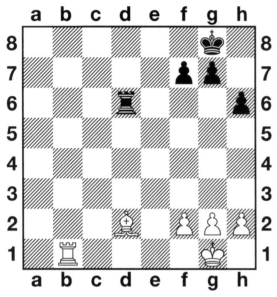

1) Black to move
Which move by Black captures a white piece for nothing?

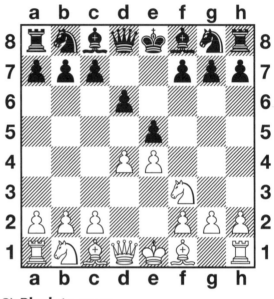

2) Black to move
Does Black have any possible captures in this position?

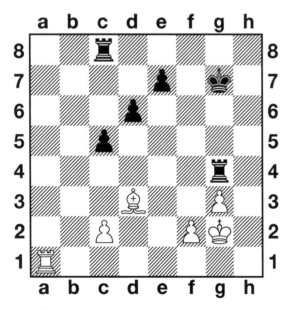

3) White to move
This is a tough one. The white bishop can move to a square where it attacks *both* black rooks at the same time. What is the bishop move?

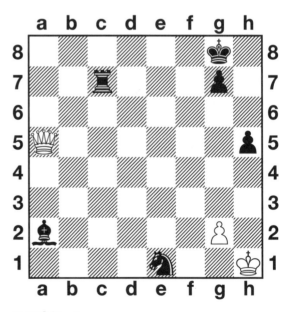

4) White to move
The white queen is attacking several undefended black pieces. She should choose the most valuable one to capture. Which piece is that?

Practicing Checks

Do Good Players Announce Check Out Loud?

*No! Although it can be fun to say "check" in friendly games,
it is not polite to announce it out loud in serious chess competitions.*

*For one thing, it might disturb other players nearby. Also, saying check out loud might be
considered an insult — implying your opponent hadn't realized his king was attacked!*

Giving Check

Because the king is so important, a threat to it is also important. We say a king is **'in check'** if it is threatened by an enemy piece or pawn.

You cannot allow your king to be captured. So if your king is in check, you **must** attend to the threat before you do anything else. It is not legal to leave your king in check.

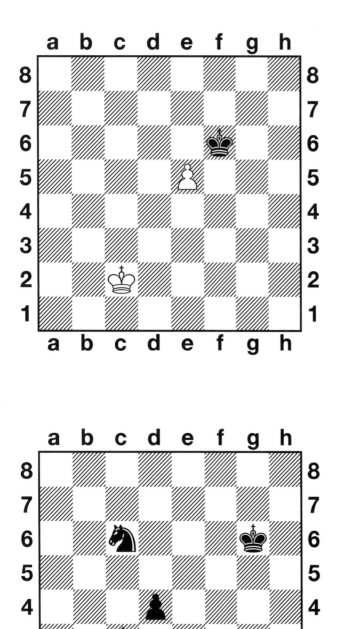

Black to move

Here the black king is **in check** from the white pawn. The pawn is attacking the black king.

But this is easily dealt with in this position. The black king (as well as moving away) could just capture the white pawn with **1...♚xe5**.

White to move

Here White is in check from a black pawn, but the situation is different. The black pawn is *protected* by the black knight. It is not legal for the white king to capture the black pawn, as this would involve moving into check.

The white king must move away.

Getting Out of Check

If you are checked, don't panic! There are three possible ways to escape from a check. It might help to remember it as **ABC**.

A   Your king might be able to move AWAY to a safer square.
B   You might be able to BLOCK the check, by putting something in the way.
C   You might be able to CAPTURE the piece giving check.

The one thing you **cannot** do is stay in check. If your king is attacked, it must escape from check immediately.

Giving Check and Escaping from Check

The next two diagrams show how a check can be **blocked**.

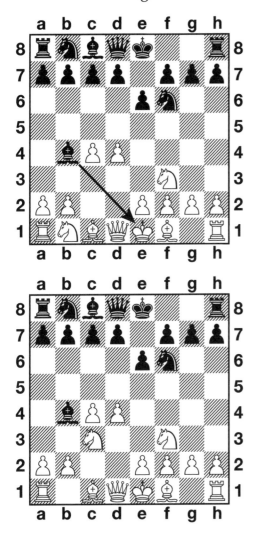

White to move

The black bishop is *checking* the white king.
The only way that White can escape from this check is to block the attack. Fortunately this is easy here. There are several white pieces that can move in the way, blocking the bishop's attack on the white king.

Black to move

Here you can see that White has chosen to block the check with his knight.

Now the knight on c3 is blocking the attack from Black's bishop. White's king is no longer in check. In this instance Black's check was not dangerous for White.

Giving Check and Escaping from Check

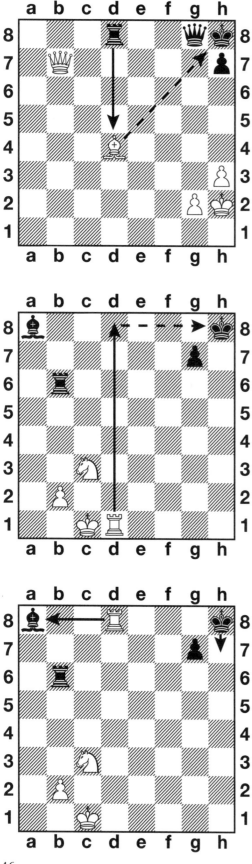

Black to move

Here you can see how to escape from check with **a capture.** The black king is in check from the white bishop. It could mean big trouble – but actually Black has one easy way to solve his problem. He can **capture the checking piece**! With 1...♖xd4 Black captures the white bishop, and so his king is no longer in check.

White to move

This and the next diagram show why checks can be so deadly. The white rook swoops down with 1 ♖d8+. This puts the black king **in check** and also attacks the black bishop. Black **must** move his king out of check. Now move on to the next diagram.

Black to move

The black king can escape from check quite easily, by moving to h7. But the check is still a disaster for Black. Why? Because now his bishop is lost. Let's see how. After the continuation 1...♔h7, White can play 2 ♖xa8 capturing the black bishop. Black **had no time to save his bishop** because he was in check.

Giving Check and Escaping from Check

It is worth remembering that a check is not always strong, but it is always a very *forcing* move. So you must always watch out for checks, and calculate the consequences carefully.

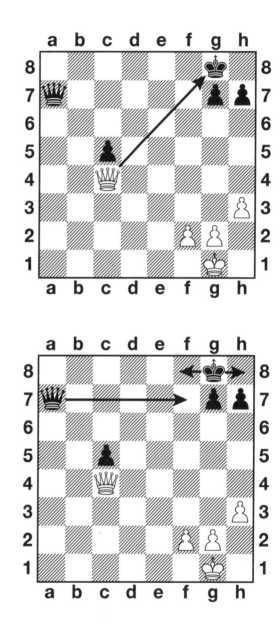

Black to move

Here White's queen has just moved to the c4 square, putting the black king *in check*. This means the black king is under attack, and must escape from check immediately.

In this position there are three possible ways for the black king to move out of check. These are shown in the next diagram.

Black to move

The arrows show the three ways that Black can escape from White's queen check in this position.

There are two ways for the black king to simply move out of check – to the f8 square or the h8 square.

The third possibility is to *block* the queen check. Black's own queen can interpose by moving to the f7 square.

How to write down "check" in algebraic chess notation...

The symbol "+" is used to show a check when writing down the moves in algebraic chess notation. For example, White's queen check in the above example would have been written ♕c4+. The white queen (♕) has moved to the c4 square giving check (+).

Win 1 point for every correct answer. Your task in these four puzzles is either to give a check or to escape from check. If you can, write down your answer in algebraic chess notation. *Solutions: page 109.*

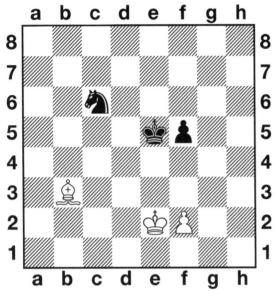

1) Black to move
Which move would put the white king in check in this position?

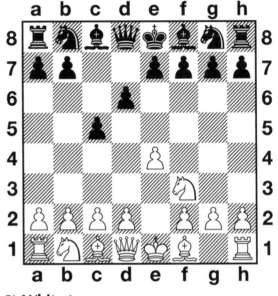

2) White to move
Which move would put the black king in check in this position?

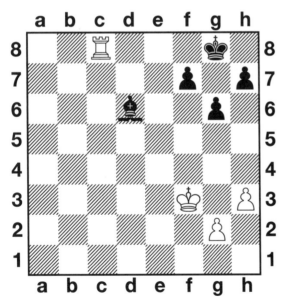

3) Black to move
The white rook is checking the black king. How many different moves does Black have to escape from this check?

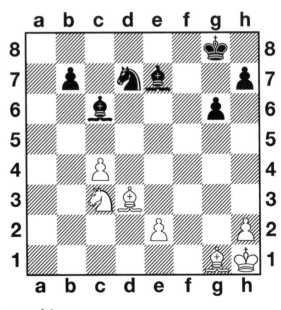

4) White to move
The black bishop on c6 is checking the white king. How many different moves does White have to block this check?

Giving Checkmate!

The aim in chess is to trap the opponent's king.
When a king is attacked, and cannot be saved, this is called checkmate.
The game is over.

Giving Checkmate!

What happens if a king is put in check, and can't escape? This is CHECKMATE! This means the end of the game. The player whose king has been checkmated has lost the game.

The whole aim of a game of chess is to trap your opponent's king. If you can reach a position where you are threatening to take your opponent's king, and there is nothing that can be done about it, then you have WON! Checkmate can happen at any time, so watch out!

Here is a beginner's checkmate trap that White can fall into in just two moves! It is called **Fool's Mate**, because it can only happen if White starts the game with two foolish moves, i.e. 1 f3 e6 2 g4.

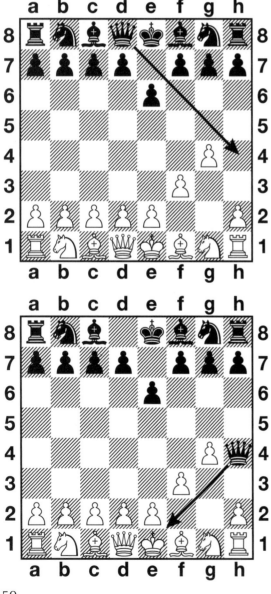

Black to move

Because White has played so poorly on his first two moves, Black can play a move here that gives instant checkmate.

The move 2...♛h4 attacks the white king. Now move on to the next diagram, and we will see why this is checkmate.

White is checkmated!

White is checkmated, because his king is under attack **and there is no escape**.

- The white king has no free squares to run to, and so cannot move out of attack.
- No white piece can block the attack.
- The piece giving check (the black queen) cannot be captured.

The game is over and Black has won.

Practicing **Checkmate!**

Do remember that **you never, ever, capture a king**. If you give checkmate the game ends immediately, so the king is not actually captured.

Many checkmates happen after one side has first won many enemy pieces. Having more pieces than your opponent is usually a big advantage. You can use your extra firepower to corner the king – and checkmate him.

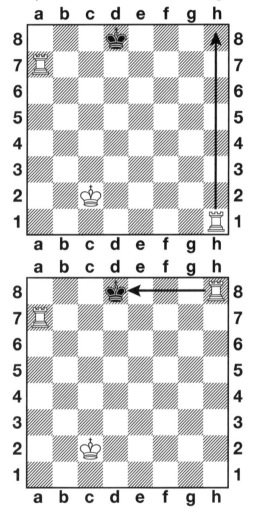

White to move

A checkmate using two rooks

White has two rooks and a king, versus the lone black king. Black is hopelessly outgunned, and it is easy for White to force checkmate with the move 1 ♖h8.

Let's move on to the next diagram to see why this is checkmate.

Black is checkmated!

You can see that the black king has been put in check by one of the white rooks. But why is this checkmate?

The reason is that the second white rook – the one on the a7 square – controls all the escape squares. The black king cannot escape from attack. White has won the game.

And a simple checkmate with a queen...

Black is in **checkmate**.

The black king is attacked, and there are no escape squares.

Can the black king capture the white queen? No! The white queen is *protected* by the white king.

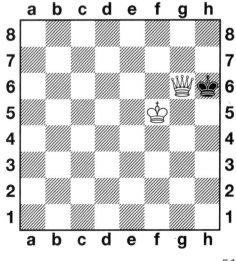

Practicing **Checkmate!**

Black to move

With a king & rook against a king, the key is to push the defending king to the edge of the board. Black checkmates with 1...♖g1.

White is checkmated

Note how White's king has been hemmed in. It cannot move forward because Black's king is controlling all the escape squares.

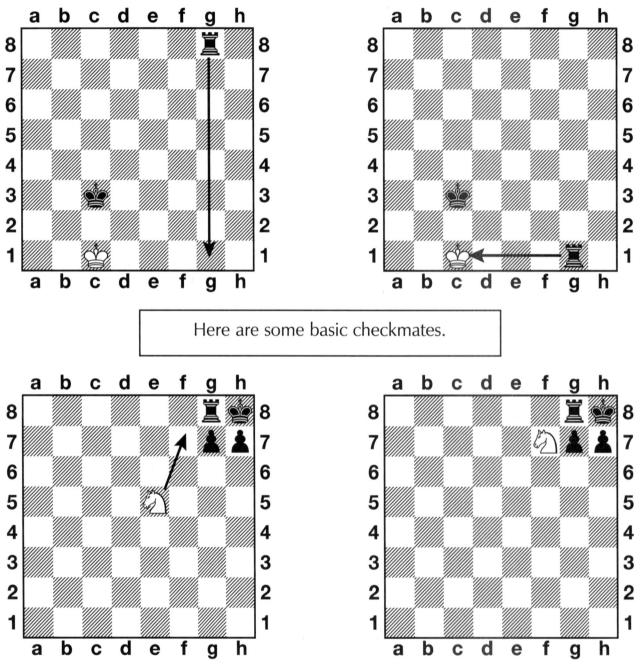

Here are some basic checkmates.

White to move

This is the beautiful "smothered mate." The escape squares for the black king are blocked by his own pieces. White plays 1 ♘f7.

Black is checkmated

Fantastic! White checkmates Black using just a single knight. The black king cannot escape as his own rook and pawns are in the way.

Practicing **Checkmate!**

White to move

The queen advance 1 ♕h7 is checkmate. Black's king is attacked – in check – and cannot escape. Let's see the next diagram.

Black is checkmated

There is nothing Black can do. The white queen cannot be captured as it is protected by the white knight on g5. The game is over – White wins!

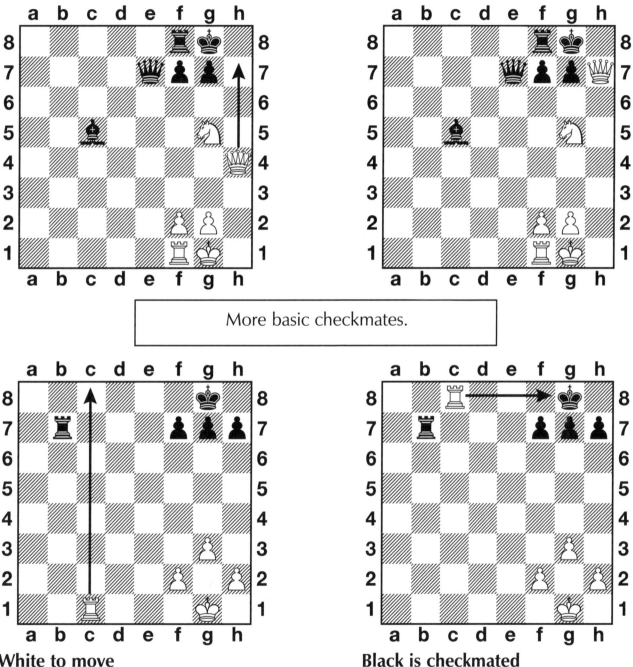

More basic checkmates.

White to move

This typical type of checkmate – where a king's escape is prevented by his own pawns – is known as a **back-rank mate**. 1 ♖c8 reaches the position in the next diagram.

Black is checkmated

The black king cannot escape the attack of the white rook. Unluckily Black's own pawns take away some of the escape squares! The game is over and White has won.

Win 1 point for every correct answer. How well can you spot the checkmates? If you can, write down your answer in algebraic chess notation. *Solutions: page 109.*

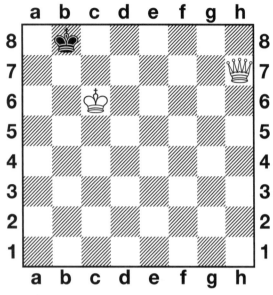

1) White to move
White is winning easily, but can you find the one move that gives immediate checkmate?

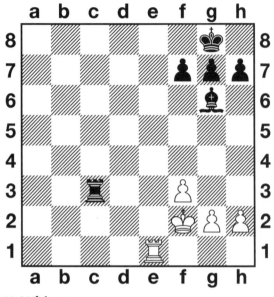

2) White to move
What is the winning move for White in this position?

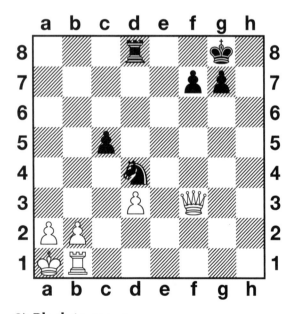

3) Black to move
Here the white queen can be won with 1...♘xf3 – but can you find an even stronger move?

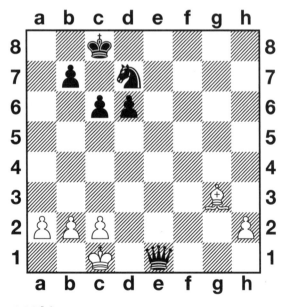

4) White to move
The white king is in check from Black's queen and cannot move. Why is this not checkmate?

PART THREE

★ **Learning to Castle** ★ **Pawn Promotion** ★ **The** *en passant* **Capture** ★

Castling involves your king, and one of your rooks.
It is the only time you get to move two of your pieces at once!

Learning to Castle

Just once in each game you are allowed to make a special move involving your king and one of your rooks. This is called 'castling.' You can castle either **kingside** or **queenside**.

It is the only time in chess that you can move two of your pieces together in a single turn. It is also the only time your king can move more than one square in a single turn.

How to Castle Kingside

Position *before* castling kingside

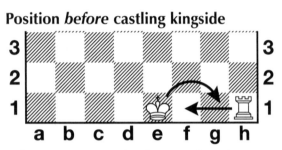

White to move. The king and rook are on their original starting squares, and there is nothing in between them.

Position *after* castling kingside

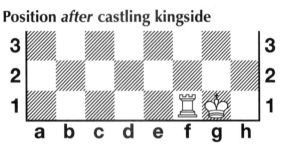

Here is the position after castling. White moved the king **two squares towards the rook**. Meanwhile, the rook has **jumped to the other side of the king**.

How to Castle Queenside

Position *before* castling queenside

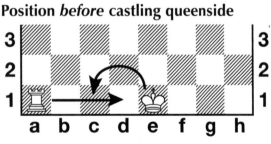

White to move. Again the king and rook are on their original squares, and there is nothing in between.

Position *after* castling queenside

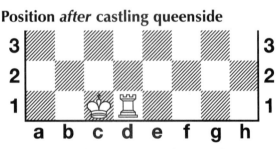

This shows the position after castling. White has moved the king **two squares towards the rook**, which itself **has jumped to the other side of the king**.

How to write down "castling" in algebraic chess notation...

Kingside castling (also called "castling short") is written as: **0-0**
Queenside castling (also called "castling long") is written as: **0-0-0**

Practicing Castling

Castling may look simple, but you have to obey a few rules to play this special move!

- You can't castle if the king or rook has already moved during the game.
- You can't castle if the king is in check, or would pass through check.
- You can't castle if the king would be in check at the end of the move.
- You can't castle if there is a piece in the way.

The first rule applies even if your king or rook has moved back to the original starting square. So if you have already moved your king – or the rook you want to castle with – you can no longer castle! You can only castle *once* during a game.

Practicing Castling

Can Black castle kingside in this position?

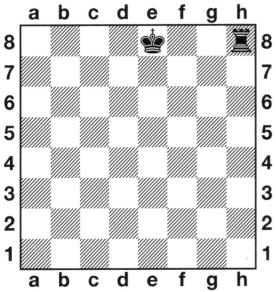

YES – provided the black king and rook have not previously moved during the game.

Can Black castle kingside in this position?

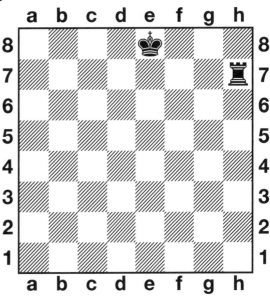

NO! The black rook is not on its original square (you can see it is on h7, instead of h8). So castling is not possible.

Practicing Castling

Can White castle kingside in this position?

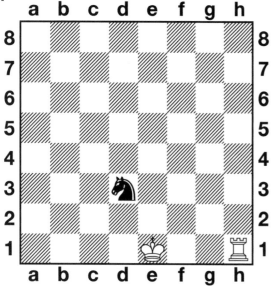

NO! White's king is IN CHECK from the black knight, so castling is illegal.

Can White castle kingside in this position?

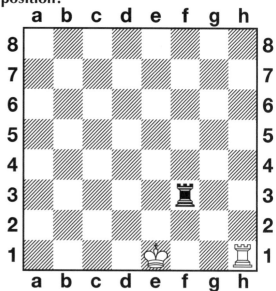

NO! White's king would have to pass through CHECK (as the black rook attacks the f1 square). This is not allowed, so White can't castle.

Can White castle queenside in this position?

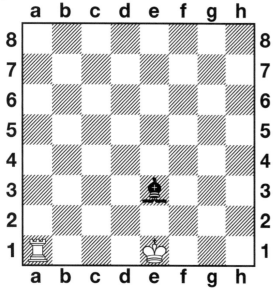

NO! After castling White's king would end up IN CHECK on the c1 square. This is not allowed, so White can't castle.

Can White castle queenside in this position?

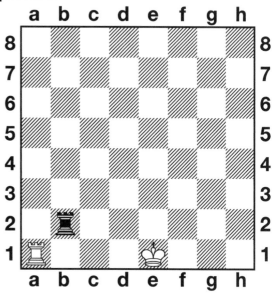

YES! A tricky one, as Black's rook controls the b1 square. But as White's KING is NOT passing through check, castling is OK.

An Example of Castling during a Game

It is good strategy to castle early. Castling removes your king from the center of the board – where there is often danger – to a much safer spot near the side of the board. Castling also means that your mighty rooks can zoom into action quickly, in the center of the board.

The next four diagrams show the start of a game where both sides castle early. The opening variation – called The Sicilian Defense – is one used by experienced players. But that doesn't matter – you can still easily play through the moves on your chessboard! Studying the games of good players is a great way to learn chess. Let's see how quickly good players like to get castled.

The starting position

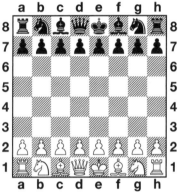

White to move
The opening moves began **1 e4 c5 2 ♘f3 d6 3 d4 cxd4 4 ♘xd4 ♘f6 5 ♘c3 ♘c6 6 ♗g5 e6 7 ♕d2 ♗e7**. Note how fast White develops most of his pieces.

Position before White castles

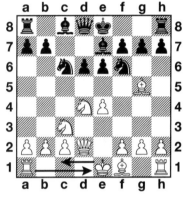

White to move
Now White is ready to castle queenside. White plays **8 0-0-0**. Remember, 0-0-0 is how we write down queenside castling in chess notation.

Position after White castles

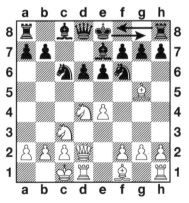

Black to move. Last move White castled, and now it is Black's turn! Black castles kingside, which we write **8...0-0**. This shows that on move 8, Black castled on the kingside.

Position after Black castles

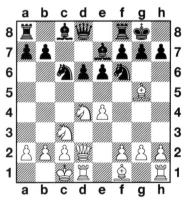

So now **both sides have castled**, early in the game too. Good opening play! The kings are safer nearer the edge of the board, and rooks are more active in the center.

Win 1 point for every correct answer. See how well you can understand the castling rules. Carefully *write down* your answer (in algebraic chess notation if appropriate). *Solutions: page 109.*

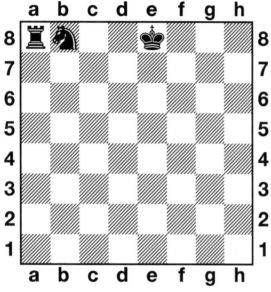

1) Can Black castle?

Here the black king and rook have never moved from their original squares. So can Black castle queenside in this position?

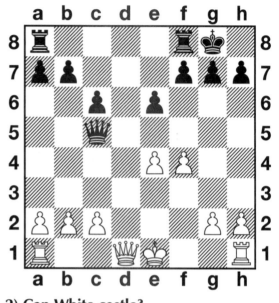

2) Can White castle?

The white king and rooks have never moved from their original squares. So can White castle kingside in this position?

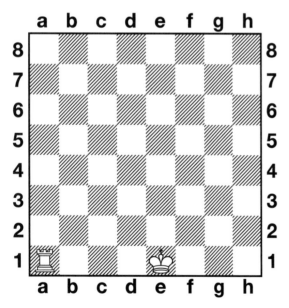

3) Where will White's rook end up?

Write down the name of the square where the *white rook* will finish up after queenside castling.

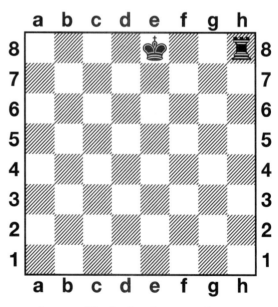

4) Where will Black's king end up?

Write down the name of the square where the *black king* will finish up after kingside castling.

Pawn Promotion

Turning a pawn into a queen is a great way to win games.

Pawn Promotion

Pawns only move forward, never backwards. So what happens when your pawn reaches the very end of the board?

In fact, something dramatic happens. A pawn which successfully reaches the eighth rank is **promoted to a piece**! Fantastic! You can choose to promote your pawn to whichever piece you like (except for a king). You could have a new queen, or rook, or bishop, or knight. However, it usually pays to promote to a new queen, as the queen is such a powerful and valuable piece. So pawn promotion is also commonly referred to as "queening a pawn."

How to Promote a Pawn to a Queen

White is about to queen the b-pawn

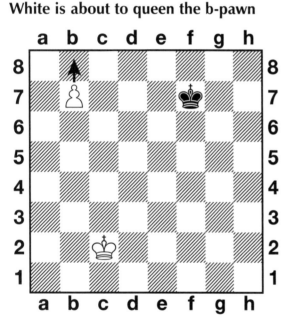

White to move. The pawn will promote if it advances one more square and reaches the eighth rank. White moves the pawn to b8 and promotes to a queen – written 1 b8=♕.

White has queened the pawn

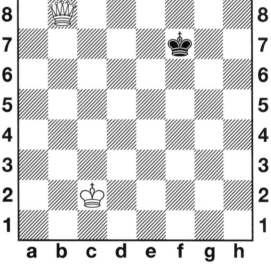

The white pawn has been taken off the board, and a white queen has been substituted. This all happens in the one move. A pawn that reaches the eighth rank must promote immediately – it cannot remain a pawn.

Practicing Pawn Promotion

Queening a pawn can often win you the game. If you can promote a lowly pawn into a powerful queen – and your opponent hasn't done the same – you have gained a huge advantage in firepower. Your new extra queen can zap around the board, capturing enemy pieces or forcing a quick checkmate.

It is unlikely an opponent will last for long if you have an extra queen on the board.

Black to move and win

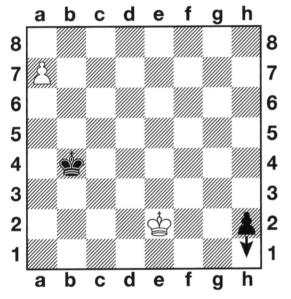

Here's an interesting position – both players have pawns poised to promote! But Black has the move, and is able to queen his pawn first with **1...h1=♕**.

White (to move) is lost

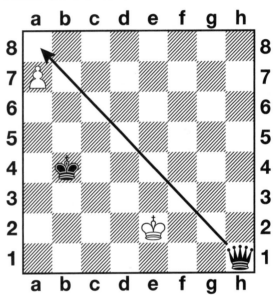

So a new black queen appears on the board. Unluckily for White, the freshly promoted black queen is covering the a8-square. If White attempted to queen his own pawn, Black could capture the new white queen.

Did you know...

Most pawn promotions occur in the *endgame* – the final part of a game, when not many pieces remain on the board. Earlier in the game there are too many pieces on the board for a pawn to successfully march all the way to the eighth rank.

How Many Queens Can I Have?

Although you start the game with only one queen, in theory you could have up to nine queens, if you promoted all eight of your pawns! But in practice it is very rare to have more than two queens.

Black (to move) gets a second queen

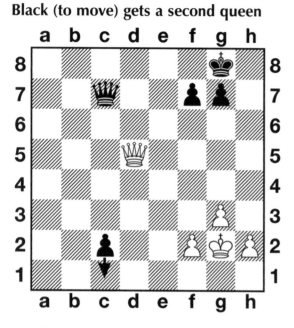

For the moment material is equal – each side has a queen and three pawns. But Black's c-pawn is very far advanced. With the move 1...c1=♕ Black promotes the pawn on c2 to a new queen.

White (to move) is lost

Now we can see that there are **two** black queens on the board, against White's one queen. The material balance is transformed! With the huge advantage of an extra queen, Black should win easily.

**White to move –
how about a PAWN RACE!**

Sometimes in simple endgame positions, a **pawn race** arises. This is where both players race a pawn towards the eighth rank, trying to be first to make a new queen.

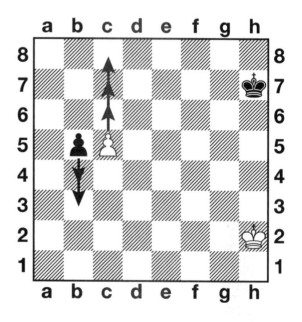

In the diagram on the right, White wins because his pawn is further advanced and it is his turn to move. After 1 c6 b4 2 c7 b3 3 c8=♕ White wins the race – and the game. With his new queen White can easily capture the black pawn before it becomes a queen.

More Pawn Promotions

White to move and win

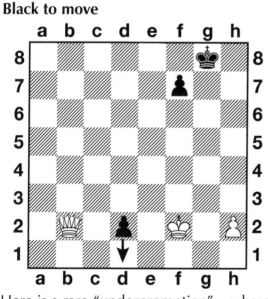

Pawns promote whenever they reach the eighth rank. This includes positions where they capture. Here White's best move is to take the black rook – promoting to a queen at the same time!

Black to move

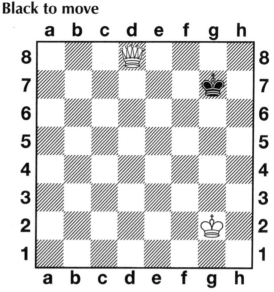

Now Black is to move. But having lost his rook – and with White having a new queen – the position is hopeless. With queen and king v king it is easy for White to force checkmate.

Underpromotion
(promoting a pawn to a piece apart from a queen)

Black to move

Here is a rare "underpromotion" – where Black chooses to promote to a knight, instead of a queen. The move 1...d1=♘+ is very clever in this position.

White (to move) is in check

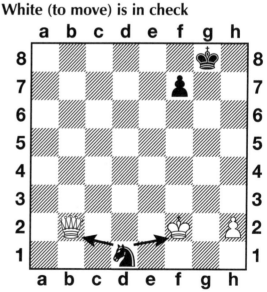

Black's underpromotion is strong because the white king and queen are simultaneously attacked. White's king must escape from check. Black then captures the white queen.

Terribly Tough Test Number Eleven

Win 1 point for every correct answer. These puzzles will test your **pawn promotion skills**. Carefully *write down* your answer (in algebraic chess notation if the answer is a chess move). *Solutions: page 109.*

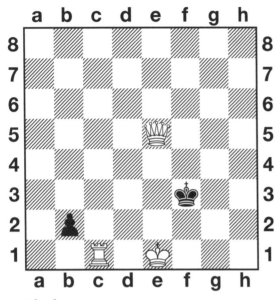

1) Black to move

A queen and a rook down, Black's position looks desperate. Can you find the saving move that checkmates White?

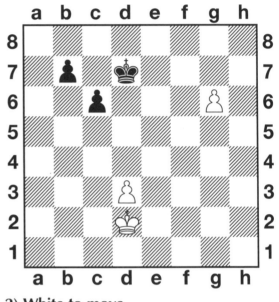

2) White to move

Each player has just two pawns and a king left. Yet White has a winning plan. What move should he play?

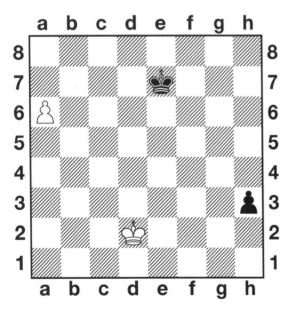

3) White to move

Both sides are in a pawn race, to see who can queen first. Who will win, White or Black?

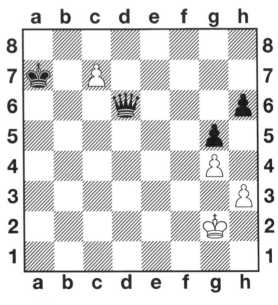

4) White to move

Is there a tricky pawn promotion that wins for White in this position?

The *en passant* Capture

Knowing the en-passant rule could save you a pot-full of trouble!

The *en passant* Capture

Even if you are only just starting, you should know about the sneaky *en passant* rule. You might trick other beginners who don't notice this pawn capture is possible! *En passant* captures only occur very occasionally. This is because only pawns can capture or be captured *en passant,* and only then in very specific situations.

Example of an *en passant* capture

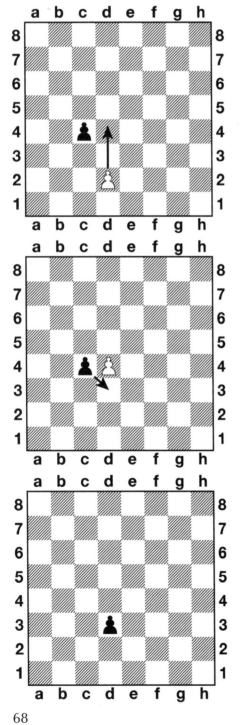

Remember the rule that allows a player to move a pawn two squares on its very first move? Well, if your opponent has a pawn of his own in the right spot, he may capture as if the enemy pawn had just moved *one* square (instead of two).

White to move

If White plays 1 d4, moving his pawn two squares, an **en passant** capture is possible by Black.

Black to move

The pawn capture 1...cxd3 is possible, pretending that the white pawn had only moved one square.

The white pawn has been captured *en passant*. The black pawn captures as though White had moved his pawn one square only.

Practicing *en passant* Captures

What does '*en passant*' mean? It is chess jargon! *En passant* is French for 'in passing.' If you take *en passant*, you are taking a pawn that is passing by.

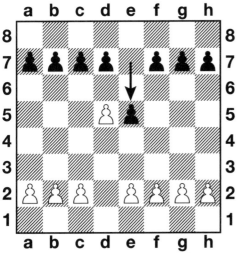

White to move. Any pawn can be captured *en passant* under the right circumstances. Last move Black advanced his e-pawn two squares forward. An *en passant* capture is now possible. White captures with 1 dxe6.

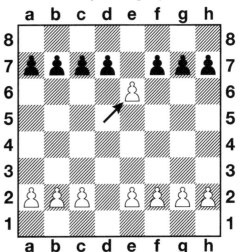

The *en passant* capture is made! White captures as though Black's pawn had only moved one square. Black's e5 pawn is removed from the board. Look where the white pawn ends up – on the e6 square.

An *en passant* capture is valid for one move only. Once an opponent has advanced his pawn two squares, you must decide **that same turn** whether to capture *en passant* or not. You can't wait and do it later.

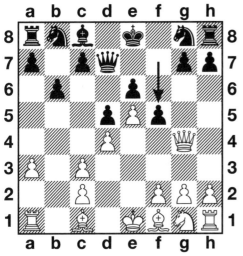

White to move. Last move Black advanced his f-pawn two squares. White can now make an *en passant* capture, written 1 exf6.

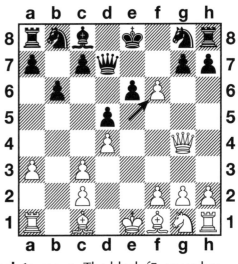

Black to move. The black f5 pawn has been captured *en passant*. Black might recapture with 1...♘xf6.

Terribly Tough Test Number Twelve

The *en passant* move is easily misunderstood by beginners, so take extra care! You win 1 point for each correct answer. Carefully write down your solution (in algebraic chess notation if appropriate). *Solutions: page 109.*

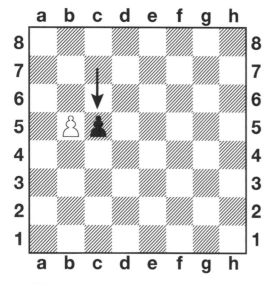

1) White to move
Last move Black advanced his pawn from its starting position with ...c5. Name the square that the *white pawn will end up on*, if White now captures *en passant*.

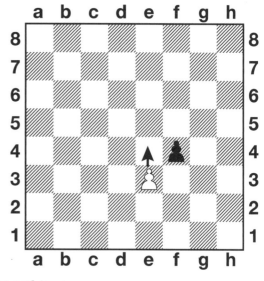

2) White to move
If White continues 1 e4 in this position, can Black capture *en passant*?

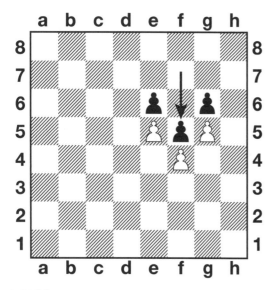

3) White to move
Black's last move was ...f5. The pawn moved from f7 to f5. How many ways does White have to capture the f-pawn *en passant*?

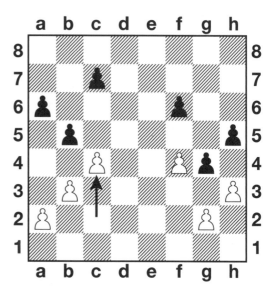

4) Black to move
White's last move was 1 c4. The pawn moved from c2 to c4. Are there any *en passant* captures possible for Black in this position?

PART FOUR

★ **How Chess Games Are Drawn** ★ **Winning Your First Games** ★

George and Kirsty would never agree a quick draw with each other.
Like mighty gladiators they would always fight to the last pawn, no matter how long it took.

Except in emergencies of course.

How Chess Games are Drawn

There are three possible outcomes to your game of chess: a win (score 1 point), a loss (score 0 points), or a DRAW, where you get half a point.

A draw is quite a normal result amongst strong chess-players – nearly one in three games ends in this way. The three most common ways that a draw comes about are:

- **Draw by Agreement**
- **Draw by Stalemate**
- **Draw by Three-fold Repetition of Position**

Draws by Agreement

If you and your opponent both want to, you can agree a draw. The game would end immediately, and if you were playing in a tournament, you would "share the point" – scoring half a point each.

You might agree a draw, for example, if you reach a completely level position with very few pieces left on the board. If it seemed that no-one was going to be able to win, one of you could offer a draw.

Did you know...
In 1978 a hard-fought draw between Anatoly Karpov and Viktor Korchnoi set a record for the longest game ever played in a World Championship. It lasted for 124 moves, and ended in a draw by stalemate. Overall the game lasted for a mammoth 12 hours and 3 minutes!

Draws by Stalemate

A stalemate occurs where one side **has no legal moves** but is **not** in check. Stalemates can seem a bit like checkmates, but there is a big difference. Because no-one is in check, a stalemate is an automatic DRAW.
Stalemates commonly occur in the endgame, when few pieces are left on the board.

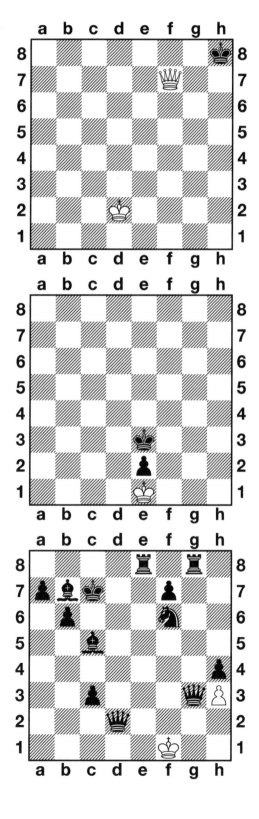

Black to move – Draw by Stalemate
Black has no pieces left apart from his king, which is cornered. White is a queen ahead, which would normally mean an easy win.

But, carelessly, White has left Black *with no legal moves*. The black king can't move to a square attacked by the white queen. So the result is a draw by stalemate – a very lucky escape for Black.

White to move – Draw by Stalemate
Some stalemates arise naturally in the endgame, not as the result of any mistake. Here White, a pawn down, has drawn by stalemate. The white king has no legal moves but is not in check.

White to move – Draw by Stalemate
Look at this crazy position. Black has nearly all of his chess pieces, and even an extra queen, but the game is drawn!

This is because Black has carelessly left White with no legal moves, yet the white king is not in check. White has a pawn, but it is blocked and can't move either. So White gets a miracle draw – by stalemate!

Practicing Stalemates

Stalemate tricks in the endgame are easy to fall into when you are learning. Even if you are winning easily – stay alert! Otherwise your opponent might swindle a draw.

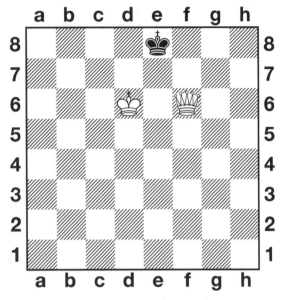

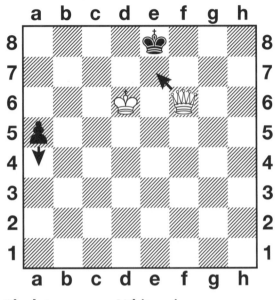

Black to move – Draw by Stalemate
The white king and queen have closed in on the lone black king, ready to give checkmate. Except, carelessly, White has stalemated Black, who has no legal moves. Draw!

Black to move – White wins
A similar position to the previous diagram. But here White has **not** allowed a stalemate, as Black still has a pawn that can move. On 1...a4, White checkmates with 2 ♕e7.

Draws by Repetition of Position

Sometimes a series of moves leads to the same position arising again and again. If the exact same position is reached three times in a game (with the same player to move) a draw may be claimed. This is an important rule, as otherwise some games might never end!

A typical draw by three-fold repetition involves "perpetual check." Perpetual check is where one player checks the enemy king repeatedly. No checkmate or other progress is possible, but the checks could go on forever!

A Draw by Repetition (involving Perpetual Check)

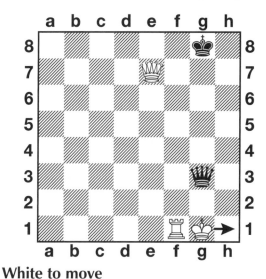

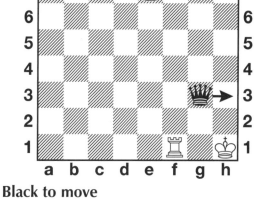

White to move

Although a rook up, White cannot escape the repeated checks from the black queen. The only move here for White's king to get out of check is 1 ♔h1, reaching the position in the next diagram.

Black to move

The checks continue: 1...♛h3+ 2 ♔g1 ♛g3+, reaching the exact position from the first diagram. Black could keep checking forever. The game will be drawn by repetition.

Two Less-Common Ways a Game can be Drawn

The "50-Move" Rule

To ensure that some games do not go on forever, there is a rule that allows a draw to be claimed *if no progress is being made*. A draw may be claimed by either player if 50 consecutive moves by both sides go by *without a pawn being moved or a capture being made*.

Insufficient Material to Win

The final way a draw can result is if neither player has enough pieces left to force checkmate under any circumstances. Then the game is an automatic draw. For example, if every single pawn and piece was swapped off, leaving just the white king and the black king remaining, the game is a draw.

Win 1 point for every correct answer. See how well you can spot the draws by perpetual check and stalemate. Carefully *write down* your answer (in algebraic chess notation if appropriate). *Solutions: page 110.*

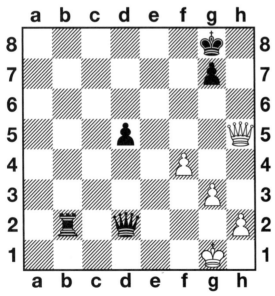

1) White to move

White is a queen ahead. Would capturing the black pawn with 1 ♕xf7 be a good move or a big mistake in this position?

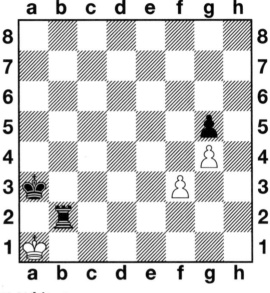

2) White to move

The white king has no legal moves, and is not in check. So is this position a draw by stalemate?

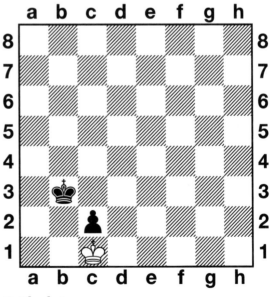

3) White to move

White is a rook down, so would be delighted with a draw. Can you see the saving move, and explain how it forces a draw?

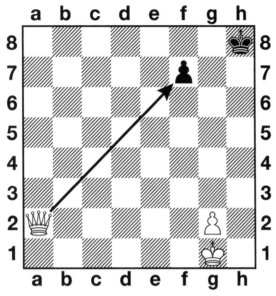

4) Black to move

The black pawn is close to queening, yet this position will be a draw very soon. Can you see why?

Winning Your First Games

The most basic winning strategy is to capture your opponent's pieces,
and then give checkmate using a queen or rooks...

Winning Your First Chess Games

So how do you win a chess game? Well, the simple answer is that you checkmate your opponent!

There are various ways to set about this. A good strategy is to first win your opponent's pieces, one by one. Eventually you will have enough extra firepower to easily force checkmate. Another way to go material ahead is to promote one of your pawns in the endgame. With an extra queen it should be simple to checkmate the enemy king.

A different winning strategy is to try a direct attack in the middlegame. By attacking your opponent's king with your pieces you might, sometimes, succeed in forcing a quick checkmate.

So, now you know some basic strategy! Now let's learn how to checkmate with an extra queen.

Mating with King & Queen against King

To achieve this checkmate, White requires the assistance of his own king to **help herd the black king to the edge of the board**. At the edge of the board there are far fewer escape squares available to the black king. The following six diagrams show a typical checkmating strategy.

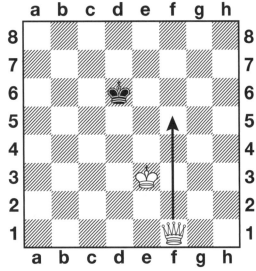

White to move
1 ♕f5 cuts down the options for the black king. After 1...♚c6 White's king advances with 2 ♔d4, to help drive the black king to the edge of the board.

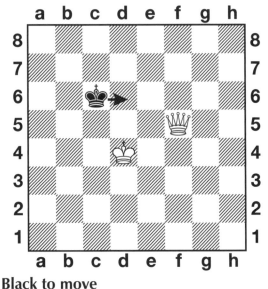

Black to move
Now 2...♚d6 3 ♕f6+ forces the black king back another rank. After 3...♚d7, 4 ♔c5! is a further clever advance of the white king.

Mating with King & Queen against King

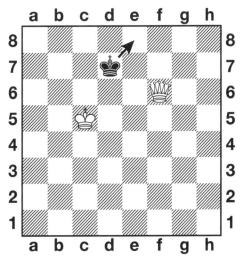

Black to move

The net is tightening (if 4...♚c7, then 5 ♕e7+ forces Black's king back still further). So Black sets a cunning stalemate trap with **4...♚e8.**

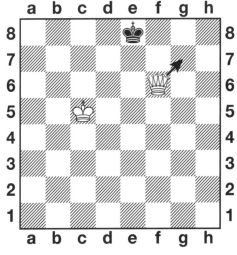

White to move

A critical moment. Don't be tempted by 5 ♚d6 or 5 ♚c6 as these blunders give Black a draw by stalemate! The key move is **5 ♕g7.**

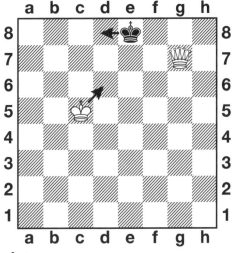

Black to move

See how the white queen has hemmed in the black king? The black king is now confined to the edge of the board. After **5...♚d8** White closes in with **6 ♚d6.**

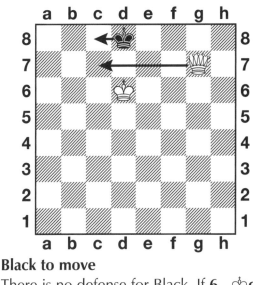

Black to move

There is no defense for Black. If **6...♚c8** White checkmates with **7 ♕c7** (or if 6...♚e8 there is a choice of checkmates, with 7 ♕e7 or 7 ♕g8).

Watch Out for those Stalemate Tricks!

With practice, you'll find it easy to mate with King & Queen v King. But concentrate hard to avoid accidentally stalemating your opponent. Remember, draws by stalemate occur where a player has no legal moves, but his king is not in check.

Mating with Queen & Rook against King

Queen and rook working together can force checkmate quickly and easily. The following four diagrams show a typical example.

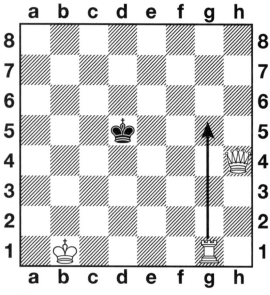

White to move

Once again the plan is to **force the black king to the edge of the board**. After **1 ♖g5+** the black king must retreat, e. g. with **1...♚d6** (it doesn't matter to which exact square).

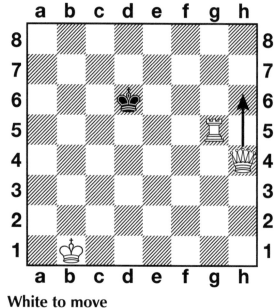

White to move

2 ♕h6+ repeats the procedure of driving back the black king. Black retreats again with **2...♚d7** (or 2...♚c7 or 2...♚e7).

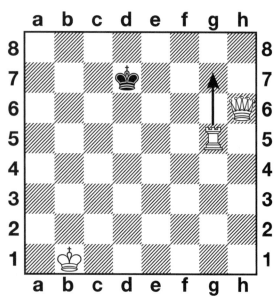

White to move

After **3 ♖g7+ ♚d8** the job is nearly done, as the black king has been forced to the edge of the board.

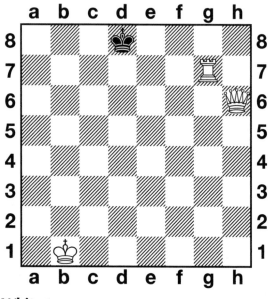

White to move

Now that Black's king can retreat no further, can you spot the killer move? Well done if you found it – **4 ♕h8 checkmate!**

Mating with Two Rooks against a King

Checkmating with two rooks uses the standard procedure of driving the king to the edge of the board. See how Black tries to obstruct matters by attacking a rook. But the long-range rooks can easily move away.

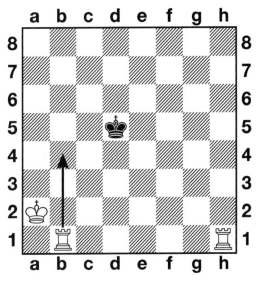

White to move
With **1 ♖b4** the rook takes control of the fourth rank, and prepares 2 ♖h5+ driving the black king back. But Black responds **1...♔c5**.

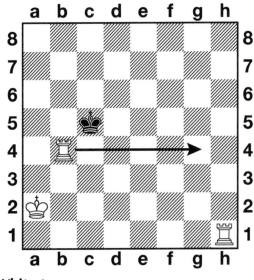

White to move
As Black's king is attacking the rook, White moves it well out of danger with **2 ♖g4**. After **2...♔d5** normal service is resumed with **3 ♖h5+ ♔e6 4 ♖g6+**.

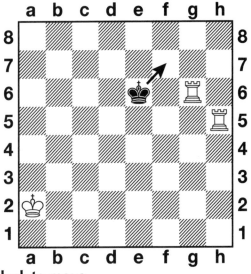

Black to move
Gradually the black king is driven back. **4...♔f7** again delays matters by attacking a rook. There follows **5 ♖a6 ♔g7 6 ♖b5** (a key maneuver) **6...♔f7**.

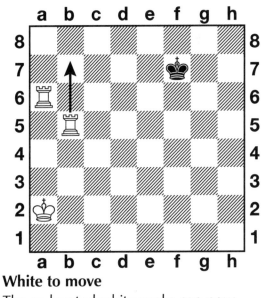

White to move
The re-located white rooks can now administer checkmate in two moves: **7 ♖b7+ ♔e8** (it is the same after 7...♔g8 or 7...♔f8) **8 ♖a8 checkmate**.

Win 1 point for every correct answer. These puzzles will test your skills at checkmating with queens and rooks. Carefully *write down* your answer (in algebraic chess notation where appropriate). *Solutions: page 110.*

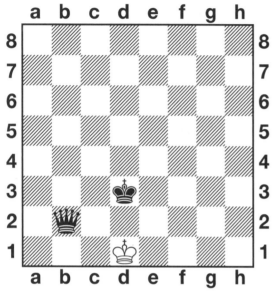

1) Black to move

The white king is trapped on the edge of the board. How many different ways can Black checkmate in one move from this position?

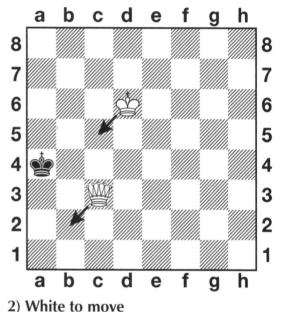

2) White to move

Here the black king is nearly trapped. Should White choose 1 ♔c5 (closing in with his own king) or 1 ♕b2 (cutting off the black king)?

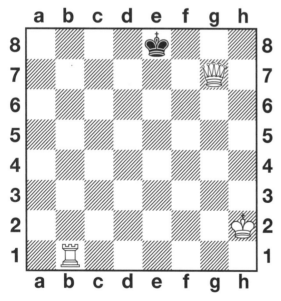

3) White to move

How does White give checkmate in one move from this position?

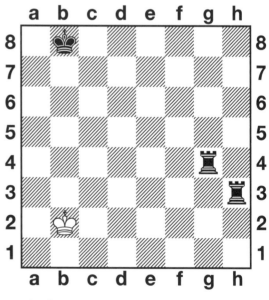

4) Black to move

How do the black rooks work in tandem to give checkmate in just two moves from this position?

PART FIVE

★ **Some Basic Tactics** ★ **How to Begin a Chess Game** ★
★ **Planning & Strategy** ★

George should have studied his chess tactics more.
In this game he'd been pinned, forked, skewered and porcupined.

Some Basic Tactics

In chess the word **tactics** means a **sequence of forcing moves** that gains an advantage. During a game both players will be constantly calculating possibilities in their heads. For example, you might be thinking "If I go there with my bishop, he captures my pawn, and then I take his rook." You are calculating tactics!

Tactics are very important, as good calculations will enable you to win material (i.e. to capture your opponent's pieces and pawns). The most frequently occurring tactical maneuvers have names, and one of the best ways to improve is to study these motifs.

The Three Most Important Tactical Motifs

★ Forks ★ Pins ★ Skewers ★

Now we are going to study these three motifs carefully. If you master these kinds of tactics, you will quickly become a stronger player.

The Fork

If you play a fork you are creating a **double attack**. One of your pieces attacks two or more vulnerable enemy pieces at the same time. You might recognize two "prongs" of a fork in the diagram below.

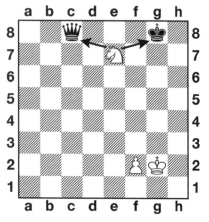

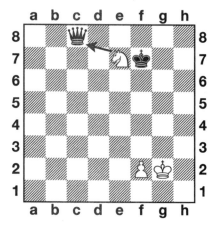

Black to move
Here is an example of a fork by the white knight. The knight is attacking two valuable black pieces at the same time (the black king and queen).

White to move
The black king was in check and so had to move. Now White can capture the black queen. The knight fork has won White a queen for nothing!

Practicing Forks

When you play a fork, it does not matter if your opponent sees that you are attacking his pieces. You will win material because you are carrying out a **double attack**. Your opponent cannot rescue both of his attacked pieces in the space of a single move.

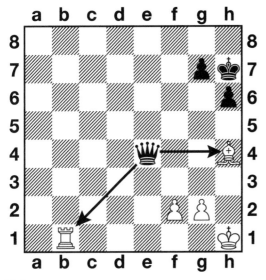

White to move

Here we see a fork by the black queen, which is attacking two undefended pieces. Even though White is to move, either the white rook or the white bishop will be lost.

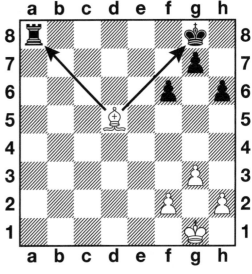

Black to move

Here the white bishop has successfully forked the black king and rook. Black must move his king out of check, after which White can capture the rook with ♗xa8.

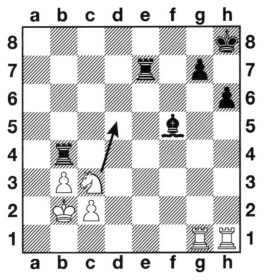

White to move

Can you spot the strong knight fork for White here? The move 1 ♘d5 attacks both black rooks (and rooks are more valuable than knights).

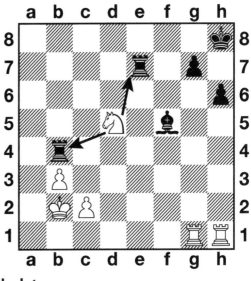

Black to move

It doesn't matter that the knight will be captured in exchange for a rook (i.e. 1...♖bb7 2 ♘xe7 ♖xe7). The swap favors White.

Pins

A **pin** occurs when a defending piece cannot move, because it would expose a more valuable piece to attack.

Some pins are almost harmless, but others are crushingly strong. Here is a gruesome example – Black is about to lose his queen for a mere bishop.

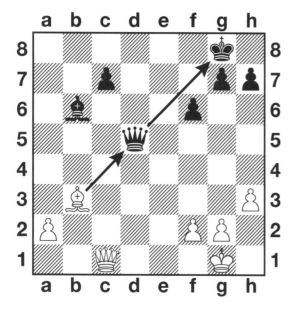

Black (to move) is pinned.
White's bishop is pinning the black queen against the black king, along the diagonal. The queen cannot sidestep the attack of the bishop, as this would expose the black king to check.

The black queen (worth 9 points) is lost.

Black will only get a white bishop (worth 3 points) in return.

More Instructive Pins

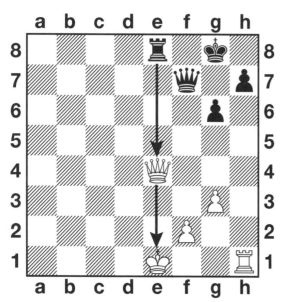

White to move
Here the white queen – under attack from the black rook – is caught in a deadly pin. The queen cannot escape as it is pinned against the king. White will lose his queen, and will only get a rook in return.

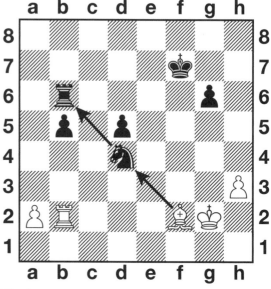

Black to move
Here the black knight is doomed. It is pinned against the black rook by the white bishop. If the knight escaped from danger by moving, then the even more valuable black rook on b6 would be lost instead.

Skewers

A **skewer** occurs where two enemy pieces are attacked along a rank, file or diagonal. When the more valuable piece in the front moves out of the way, the piece behind is captured.

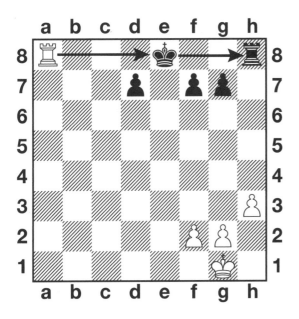

Black (to move) is skewered.

This is a common type of skewer, in which Black loses a rook for nothing.

The black king is in check from the white rook, and must move. But after 1...♔e7, White has 2 ♖xh8, winning the black rook for nothing.

A simple bishop skewer

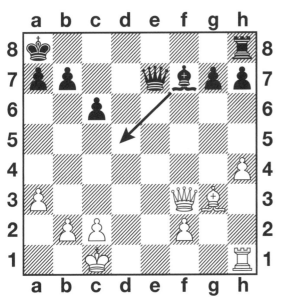

Black to move

Bishops are great at skewering! In this position material is level (each side has a queen, rook, bishop and five pawns). But Black plays 1...♗d5, cruelly skewering White's queen and rook.

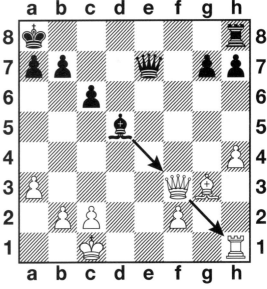

White to move

Naturally White will save his valuable queen, at the cost of allowing his rook to be captured. After 2 ♕d1 ♗xh1 3 ♕xh1 Black has successfully gained a rook (worth 5 points) for a bishop (worth 3 points).

Chess tactics are the key to winning pieces and pawns. Award yourself 1 point for every correct answer. Carefully *write down* your answer in algebraic chess notation. *Solutions: page 110.*

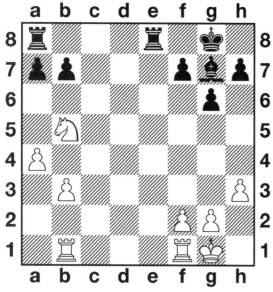

1) White to move

Can you spot a strong knight fork for White in this position?

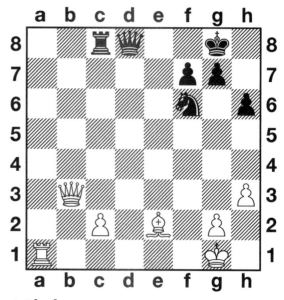

2) Black to move

What is the winning queen fork that Black can play in this position?

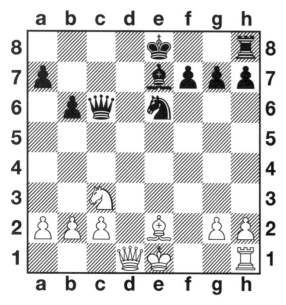

3) White to move

There is a move that pins and wins the black queen in this position. Which move?

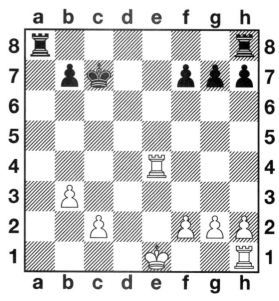

4) Black to move

What is Black's winning move in this position?

How to Begin a Chess Game

*Kirsty's new move in the Dragon variation was
definitely going to surprise George.*

How to Begin a Chess Game

The first part of a game of chess is called the opening. There many different possible chess openings, but the objectives are usually the same:

★ **to develop the pieces ready for action** ★
★ **to control the center of the board** ★
★ **to castle the king to safety** ★

In the starting position of a game, your own pawns severely restrict the movement of your pieces (the knights, bishops, rooks and the queen). So to develop these pieces onto useful squares, some pawn moves must first be made. It is useful if these pawn moves can also **claim some territory in the center of the board**. Control of the center is desirable, as it enables your pieces to work together better.

Let's look at an example of a chess opening which illustrates these ideas in action.

A Sample Chess Opening
(the "French Defense")

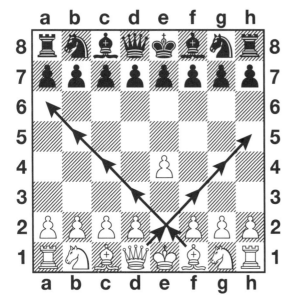

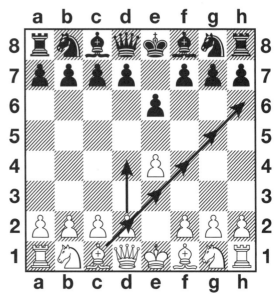

White has played **1 e4**. This typical first move immediately activates some white pieces. White's queen and bishop – hemmed in before – now both have several squares they could potentially move to later on.

Black has chosen **1...e6**, an opening move called the *French Defense*. White now replies **2 d4**, another pawn advance that seizes territory in the center. The white bishop on c1 is also activated.

A Sample Chess Opening

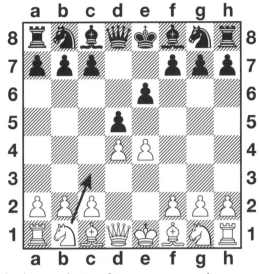

Black's reply **2...d5** was a central counter-attack with his own pawn. Now White's **3 ♘c3** has a dual purpose. The knight develops to an active square near the center. It also defends the attacked pawn on e4.

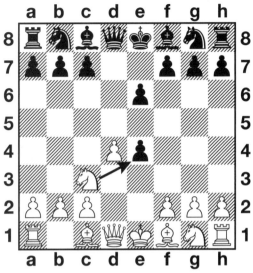

Black has swapped pawns with **3...dxe4**, and White is about to recapture with **4 ♘xe4**. Next, both sides continue with piece development: **4...♘d7 5 ♘f3 ♘gf6 6 ♘xf6+** (a knight swap) **6...♘xf6 7 ♗d3**.

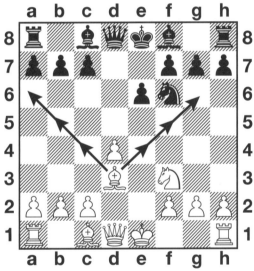

See how well-placed the white bishop is on the d3 square, where it controls lots of squares. Now after Black's **7...♗e7** White is ready to castle his king to safety with **8 0-0**.

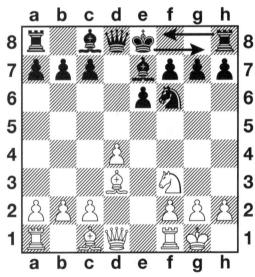

After Black now castles with **8...0-0** the opening stage is mostly over. White's next move might be 9 ♖e1, 9 ♗g5, or 9 ♕e2 – all good piece-developing moves.

As these *French Defense* moves show, in some openings there is not much immediate contact between the white and black forces. Apart from a couple of swaps (a pawn and a knight each), both sides concentrated on controlling the center, and on getting their pieces developed.

A Dream Opening Position

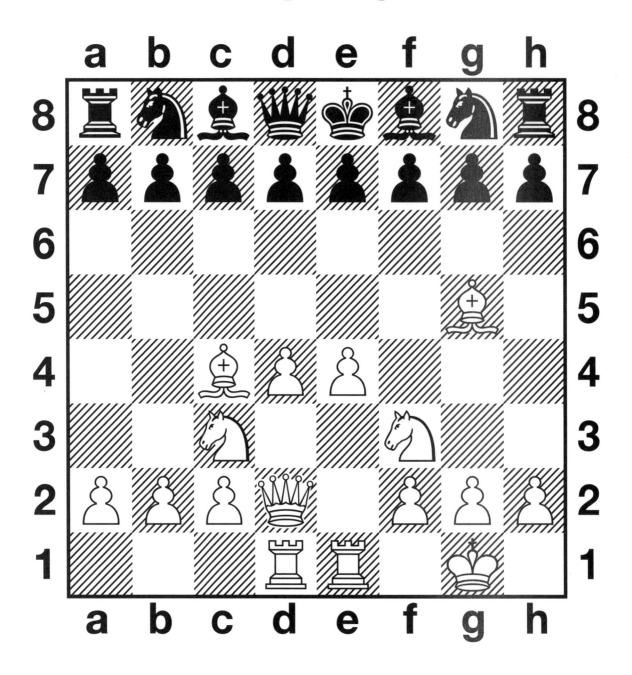

This position shows an ideal opening development of the white pieces.

- The white pawns on e4 and d4 occupy the center
- The white bishops and knights are actively placed and also control central squares
- The white queen is developed (but not so far out as to be exposed to any danger).
- The two white rooks exert pressure down the central e- and d-files
- White's king is castled to safety

An Opening Trap to Avoid

As you are just learning chess, some of your friends might try to trap you with a sneaky opening known as **Scholar's Mate**. If you are not careful you could be checkmated in only four moves! In a Scholar's Mate, White aims for a lightning-quick attack against the f7 square with his queen.

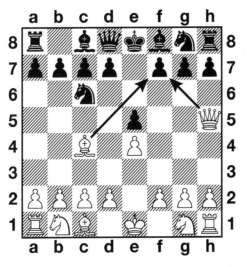

The opening moves were **1 e4 e5 2 ♕h5 ♘c6 3 ♗c4**. White is attacking the f7 square with both queen and bishop. Let's see what happens if Black overlooks the threat and plays a move like **3...d6**.

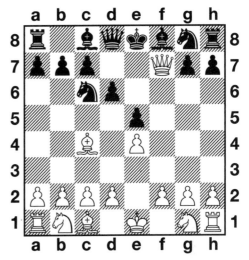

A disaster for Black has occurred! The white queen has captured with **4 ♕xf7**, giving **checkmate**. The queen is protected by the white bishop, so there is nothing Black can do.

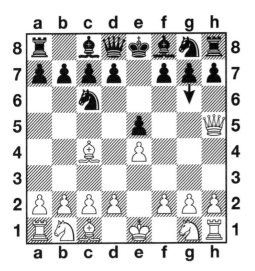

Fortunately, if you are playing Black, it is easy to stop Scholar's Mate. One way is to block the white queen's attack against the f7 square. In this position, **3...g6** blocks the attack – and threatens the white queen. On **4 ♕f3** (attacking f7 again) the move **4...♘f6** safely blocks the attack once more.

If your friends try to trap you with Scholar's Mate, you should be happy! This is because it is not really a good opening for White. **The white queen is developed too early** and a queen developed too early in the opening is easily attacked by enemy pieces. Provided you don't fall for the checkmate, you should gain a nice position.

Some Different Ways to Open a Chess Game

There are many different chess openings. Here are the names and moves of a few of the most popular ones.

QUEEN PAWN OPENINGS

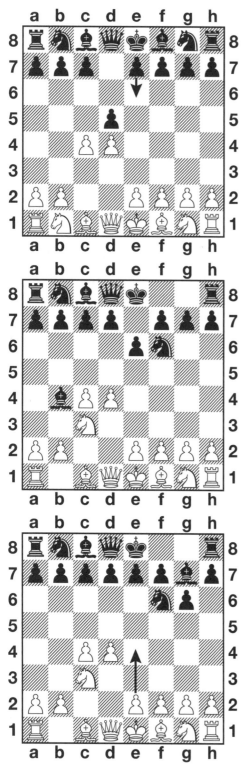

The Queen's Gambit

1 d4 d5 2 c4

White offers to give up a pawn — a "sacrifice" — but usually Black declines with the solid reply 2...e6.

The Nimzo-Indian Defense

1 d4 ♞f6 2 c4 e6 3 ♞c3 ♝b4

A counter-attacking system. Black immediately brings out his bishop and *pins* the white knight!

The King's Indian Defense

1 d4 ♞f6 2 c4 g6 3 ♞c3 ♝g7

Black is tempting White to build a big pawn center with 4 e4. Will that big center be strong or weak? An exciting system!

Some Different Ways to Open a Chess Game

KING PAWN OPENINGS

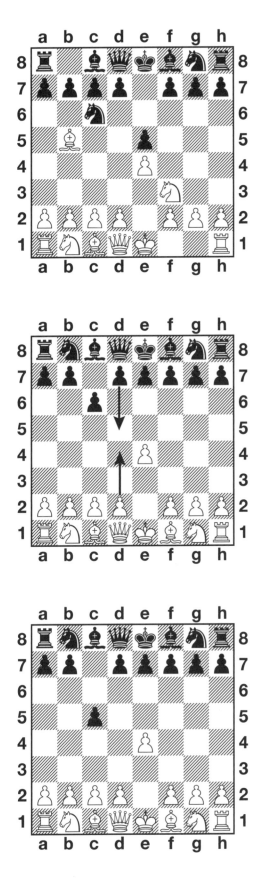

The Ruy Lopez

1 e4 e5 2 ♘f3 ♘c6 3 ♗b5

This old favorite has been popular for 150 years. It often results in a complex and blocked kind of game.

The Caro-Kann Defense

1 e4 c6

Regarded as a solid way to open. The most common follow-up goes 2 d4 d5.

The Sicilian Defense

1 e4 c5

A hugely exciting defense. One crazy line starts 2 ♘f3 d6 3 d4 cxd4 4 ♘xd4 ♘f6 5 ♘c3 g6 – the Dragon variation!

See how well you have mastered some basic opening ideas. You win 1 point for every correct answer. Carefully *write down* your answer (in algebraic chess notation if appropriate). *Solutions: page 110.*

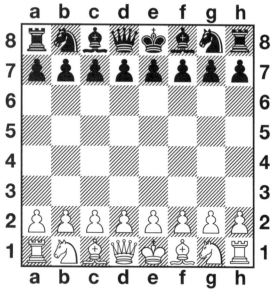

1) White to move

You are ready to make your first move. If you had to choose between playing 1 e4 or 1 h3, which pawn move would be best?

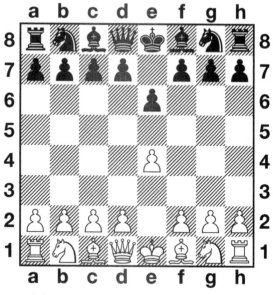

2) White to move

The game has started **1 e4 e6**. Can you give the *name* of the opening variation that Black is defending with?

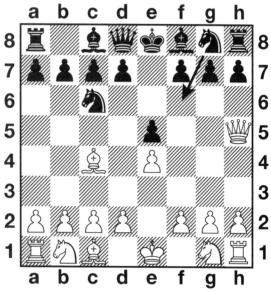

3) Black to move

One of your friends has tried to trick you into a Scholar's Mate. Is 3...♘f6 (attacking the white queen) a good defense in this position?

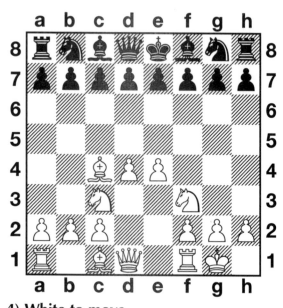

4) White to move

Who do you think has the better position, White or Black? To get your point you need to explain the reason.

Planning & Strategy

Playing chess makes you think ahead. It is a challenge to plot clever strategies to outwit your opponent.
Watching chess is fun too — you can practice working out the best plans for both players.

Planning & Strategy

After 10–15 moves have been played, both players have usually finished developing their pieces. The *opening* stage is over, and the *middlegame* begins. The middlegame calls for clever maneuvering, as both players try and gain small advantages in position.

Top Middlegame Strategy Tips

- Keep a look out for a *combination* – a series of forcing moves – that might win you pawns or pieces.

- Consider if a direct attack on the enemy king might work. Sometimes you can sacrifice your own pawns and pieces if you can get at the enemy king.

- If there are no immediate combinations or attacks possible, just maneuver your pieces into effective positions.

- Keep your king safe! In the opening or middlegame your king should hide behind your own pawns and pieces for protection.

- *One of the most important things is to think ahead! Try to anticipate what your opponent might play in response to your moves.*

Here is an example of a successful middlegame attack

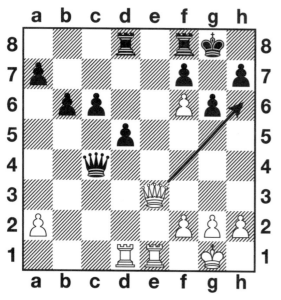

White to move

Here White has very few pieces near the black king. But surprisingly a direct checkmating attack is still possible.

1 ♕h6

This strong move wins instantly for White. The deadly threat is 2 ♕g7 checkmate next move (as the queen is protected by the white pawn on f6). Even though it is Black's turn to move, there is nothing he can do to prevent White's threatened checkmate.

A Combination to Win Material

Here is a simple example of a *combination* to win material. The question is: should White capture the black pawn on d5 with his knight? At first it seems this pawn is defended by Black's own knight. But wait – look how White's rook is also helping to attack the d5-pawn! White has more pieces attacking the d5-pawn than Black has defending it. White can win the pawn!

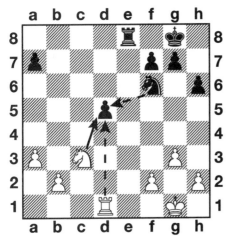

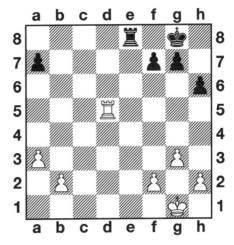

White to move
After the capture 1 ♘xd5 it is true that Black can recapture the white knight with 1...♘xd5. However, White can in turn recapture the black knight with 2 ♖xd5.

White has won a pawn
Let's work out what has happened. White has captured a pawn and a knight. Black has captured just a knight. So the combination has won White a pawn.

Endgame Strategy – Use the King Actively

We have seen that king safety is very important in the middlegame – your king must shelter behind pawns for protection. However, a transformation takes place once the endgame is reached. In endgames there are few dangerous pieces left on the board. *This means your king can – and should – be used actively.*

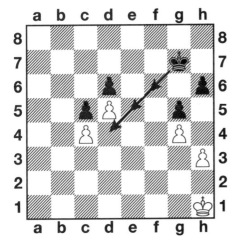

Black to move
In this pawn endgame, the winning strategy is for the black king to march right up the board! It is perfectly safe for the king to take an active role here, as the powerful pieces of both players have all been swapped off.

Play might go 1...♚f6 2 ♔g2 ♚e5 3 ♔f3 ♚d4. Next move the bold black king will capture the white pawn on c4 for nothing, giving a winning advantage.

These final positions are an inspirational challenge – the puzzles all come from games played in international chess tournaments! Your task is to find the dazzling sacrificial combination that forced a quick checkmate, or won material. Take 1 point for every correct answer, carefully *writing down* your answer in algebraic chess notation. *Solutions: page 110.*

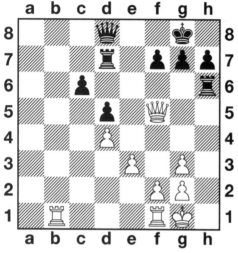

1) White to move

Although material is level, White has a queen sacrifice offer that wins here. But you'll need to calculate two or three moves ahead!

2) White to move

Remember on page 98 how White forced checkmate with just a queen and pawn? You can use a similar idea here – if you find a brilliant first move.

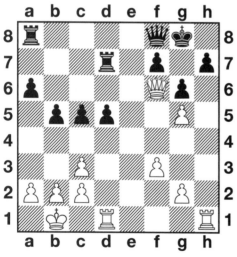

3) White to move

There are some powerful white pieces near the black king. Can you calculate a winning rook sacrifice that strips away the black king's pawn shelter?

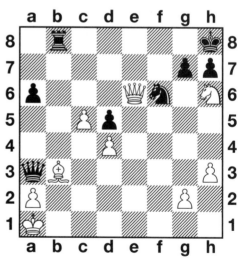

4) White to move

This final puzzle features one of the most beautiful checkmating themes in chess – the *smothered mate*! How does White force checkmate in just two moves?

PART SIX

Kirsty v George
The BIG MATCH

*A great way to improve is to sit down with your chess set,
and play over the games of strong players.
You now know how to do this!
Make each move on the board as you read through the chess notation,
and study the game, one move at a time.*

The Big Match: Kirsty and George Play a Game

Here is a complete game of chess to practice on: the big match between alligator and pupil! Is Kirsty really the Grand Alligator of chess that she claims to be? Find out by playing over the following brilliantly played game...

Kirsty (white) v George (black)
Opening variation: *Sicilian Accelerated Dragon*

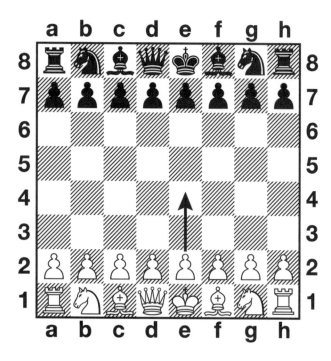

1 e4   **...**

"There, that's my first move," said Kirsty, moving her white e-pawn two squares forward. "What do you think of that!"

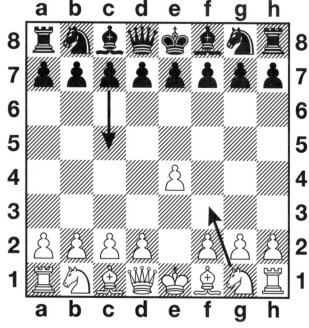

"The old King's Pawn Game, eh?" said George. "Well I know just the move to deal with this – the deadly Sicilian Defense!"

1 ...   **c5**

"That's brave," said Kirsty. "Do you mind if I move my white knight out to put pressure on the center?"

2 ♘f3   **...**

The Big Match: Kirsty and George Play a Game

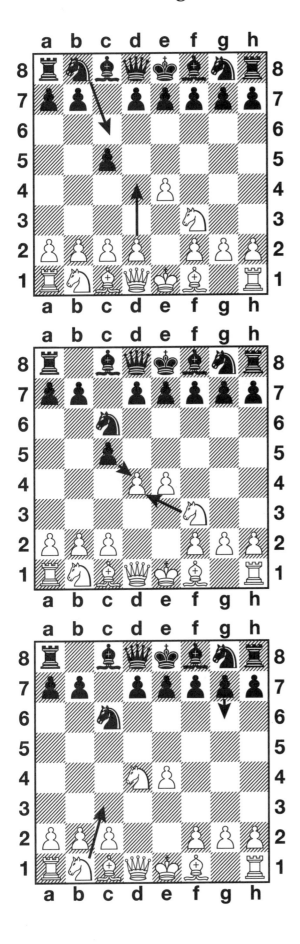

"Not at all," said George. "Because my black knight is coming out to do exactly the same."

2 ...   ♘c6

"The white d-pawn advances, which opens useful lines for pieces like my bishop and queen," said Kirsty. "This is all well-known from my famous book, Alligator Chess Openings."

3 d4   ...

"You can't fool me," said George. "I can see you are attacking my pawn. So I'm going to capture your pawn first."

3 ...   cxd4

"As ACO says," said Kirsty, recapturing the pawn on d4 with her white knight, "it's only a swap, a pawn for a pawn. Would you like to buy a copy?"

4 ♘xd4   ...

"Not needed," said George, pushing his g7 pawn to the g6 square. "It won't have this variation – I've just invented it! It's the super-duper hyper-advanced ultra-accelerated Dragon system."

4 ...   g6

"Hmm," said Kirsty. "Perhaps, Grasshopper, I have taught you too well. I'd better play a nice safe move and develop my white knight."

5 ♘c3   ...

103

The Big Match: Kirsty and George Play a Game

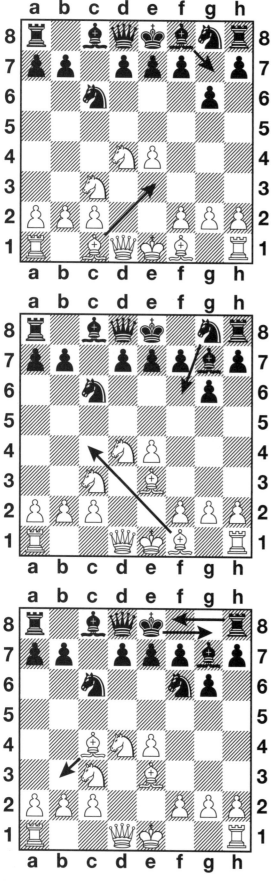

"Then I'll develop my bishop," said George, moving instantly.

5 ...   ♗**g7**

"I note your cunning attack on my d4 knight," said Kirsty. "Fortunately I can protect it at the same time as developing my bishop to an active square."

6 ♗e3   **...**

"Well, my pieces are developing to active squares just as fast as yours," said George. "Look: after my knight moves I'm even ready to castle."

6 ...   ♘**f6**

"Castle early and often – the family motto," said Kirsty. "Just what do you think of this c4 square? Isn't it a great active spot for my bishop to sit on?"

7 ♗c4   **...**

George was preoccupied. "How does that useful castling move go again?" he wondered. "Oh, that's right – the king moves two squares, and the rook comes to the other side. Easy!"

7 ...   **0-0**

Kirsty was thinking hard. "A little bishop retreat is called for, I think," she said after a few minutes' thought.

8 ♗b3   **...**

The Big Match: Kirsty and George Play a Game

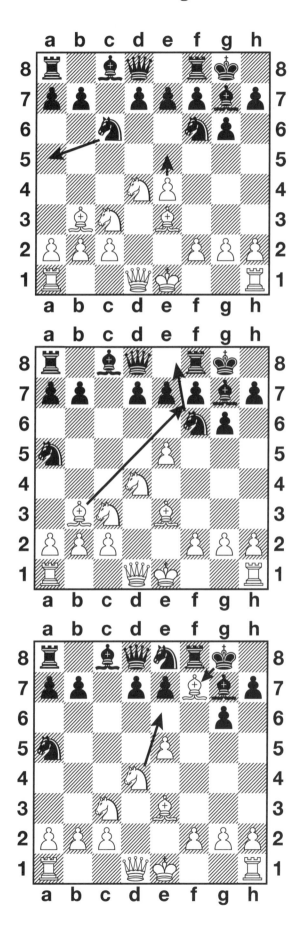

"Retreating already! What a wimpish move," said George, moving his knight to attack the bishop. He could tell Kirsty was rattled, because she was taking so long to move.

8 ...   ♘a5

"My e-pawn advances to attack your other knight," said Kirsty. "How about a little swap – my pawn for your knight?"

9 e5   ...

"No way!" said George, hurriedly moving his knight out of danger. "My knight is worth three times as much as your pawn."

9 ...   ♘e8

"Bishop takes the f7 pawn – check!" announced Kirsty.

10 ♗xf7+   ...

"What a blunder!" laughed George. "King takes bishop. I've won your bishop for just one pawn."

10 ...   ♚xf7

"Oh dear," said Kirsty, suddenly concentrating very hard. "Well how about this knight move, attacking your queen?"

11 ♘e6   ...

The Big Match: Kirsty and George Play a Game

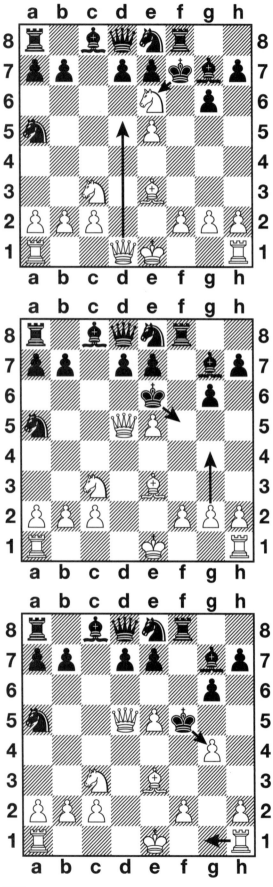

"Call yourself a Grand Alligator of chess do you?" laughed George. "Now I can capture your knight for free with my king."

11 ...   ♔xe6

"Check," announced Kirsty, moving her queen to the d5 square.

12 ♕d5+   ...

"Big deal," said George. "I'll just move my king out of check. I've got an extra bishop and knight, so I must be winning easily."

12 ...   ♔f5

"Check again," announced Kirsty, advancing the white g-pawn two squares.

13 g4+   ...

"Now you've lost a pawn as well," hooted George. "King takes pawn."

13 ...   ♔xg4

"Rook to g1 – it's check again," said Kirsty.

14 ♖g1+   ...

The Big Match: Kirsty and George Play a Game

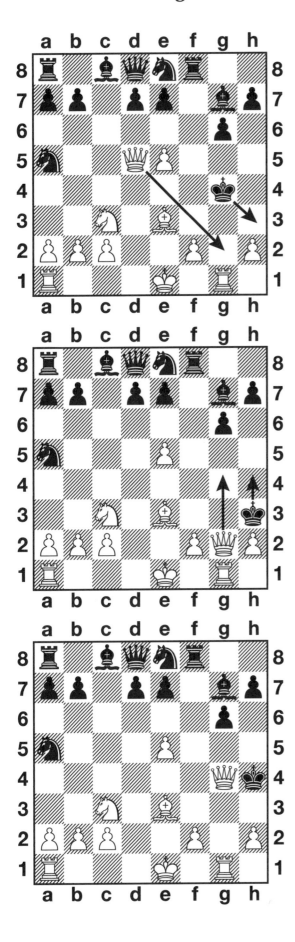

"OK, my king is a tiny bit exposed in enemy territory," said George. "But I can just move out of check. And look at all that extra material I have won. Why don't you just resign, Kirsty?"

14 ...   ♔**h3**

"Check," announced Kirsty, moving her queen to the g2 square.

15 ♕g2+   **...**

"That is a lot of checks," said George. "But my king still has a free square to move to."

15 ...   ♔**h4**

"And now this final white queen move," said Kirsty, "gives CHECKMATE. Your king is attacked and can't escape. You can't capture my queen, because it is protected by my rook. You are a bishop and knight up, but you've lost the game!"

16 ♕g4 CHECKMATE

George stared at the checkmate on the chessboard, and suddenly smiled. He realized that chess was easy to learn, but hard to master!

Luckily he had a famous Grand Alligator of chess to help teach him.

Solutions to Terribly Tough Tests

Take one point for each correct answer. You can keep score by ticking a box on the right-hand side of each answer with a pencil. At the end of each part, add up your score and see how well you did!

PART ONE

	Terribly wrong (no points)	Terribly right (one point)

Terribly Tough Test Number One (from page 8)
1) A **white bishop** and a **black king**.
2) The four **ROOKS** are missing.
3) There are **16 pawns** (eight white and eight black).
4) There are **four knights** (two white and two black).

Terribly Tough Test Number Two (from page 12)
1) The **black pawn**.
2) **No**. The black pawn is in the way.
3) **Two pieces** (the black queen and the black bishop).
4) The **white pawn**.

Terribly Tough Test Number Three (from page 16)
1) **Two pieces** (the black bishop and the black rook).
2) **No**. The white pawn is in the way.
3) **Yes**, the white king can capture the black knight.
4) The black king has **only one legal move** here (sideways).

Terribly Tough Test Number Four (from page 20)
1) **No**. A pawn can only move two squares from its *starting* position.
2) The **white rook**.
3) The **black rook**.
4) The knight attacks *three* pieces (White's bishop, queen and rook).

Now Add up Your Points for Part One

All 16	Grand Alligator Standard		12-15	Excellent!		8-11	Very Good
4-7	Average		0-3	More practice needed			

PART TWO

	Terribly wrong (no points)	Terribly right (one point)

Terribly Tough Test Number Five (from page 30)
1) **1 d4**. The "1" shows it is move one; "d4" is the pawn's arrival square.
2) **1... ♖c2**. The rook moves to the c2 square.
3) **1 ♘xc6**. The knight captures on the c6 square.
4) **1...♗xb2**. The bishop captures on the b2 square.

Terribly Tough Test Number Six (from page 34)
1) It is a **bad trade**. White loses a knight (value three pawns) for only one pawn.
2) The swap is **equal**. Each player has captured a bishop.
3) Black should capture the **white rook** (worth five pawns).
4) Swapping a queen (worth nine pawns) for a rook (worth five pawns) is a **very bad trade**.

Terribly Tough Test Number Seven (from page 42)
1) **1... ♖xd2**.
2) Yes, Black has the capture **1...exd4**.
3) **1 ♗f5**.
4) The queen should capture the **black rook**.

PART TWO (Continued)

	Terribly wrong (no points)	Terribly right (one point)

Terribly Tough Test Number Eight (from page 48)
1) **1...♘d4+** puts the white king in check from the black knight. ☐ ☐
2) **1 ♗b5+** puts the black king in check from the white bishop. ☐ ☐
3) There are **two** ways to get out of check: 1...♗f8 or 1...♔g7. ☐ ☐
4) There are **four** ways to block the check: ♘d5, ♘e4, ♗e4 or the pawn move e4. ☐ ☐

Terribly Tough Test Number Nine (from page 54)
1) **1 ♕b7** is checkmate. ☐ ☐
2) **1 ♖e8** is checkmate on the back rank. ☐ ☐
3) Black should prefer **1...♘c2 checkmate**! ☐ ☐
4) It is not checkmate as **Black's queen can be captured** with **1 ♗xe1**. ☐ ☐

Now Add up Your Points for Part Two

All 20	Grand Alligator Standard	16-19	Excellent!	10-15	Very Good
5-9	Average	0-4	More practice needed		

PART THREE

	Terribly wrong (no points)	Terribly right (one point)

Terribly Tough Test Number Ten (from page 60)
1) **No**. Black cannot castle because his knight is in the way. ☐ ☐
2) **No**. The g1 square is attacked by Black's queen. ☐ ☐
3) The **d1 square**. ☐ ☐
4) The **g8 square**. ☐ ☐

Terribly Tough Test Number Eleven (from page 66)
1) Black wins by **1...bxc1=♕ checkmate** – simultaneously capturing a rook and promoting to a new queen. ☐ ☐
2) **1 g7** wins easily: Black's king is too far away to stop the pawn promoting next move. ☐ ☐
3) **White wins** with 1 a7 h2 2 a8=♕. The new white queen now controls Black's potential queening square. ☐ ☐
4) Underpromotion to a knight with **1 c8=♘+** wins. The black king and queen are both under attack. ☐ ☐

Terribly Tough Test Number Twelve (from page 70)
1) The white pawn ends up on the **c6** square. ☐ ☐
2) **No**. As White's pawn has advanced from the e3 square (instead of the e2 square), an *en passant* capture is not legal. ☐ ☐
3) There are **two** ways to capture *en passant* here: 1 exf6 or 1 gxf6. ☐ ☐
4) **No**. ☐ ☐

Now Add up Your Points for Part Three

All 12	Grand Alligator Standard	9-11	Excellent!	6-8	Very Good
3-5	Average	0-2	More practice needed		

PART FOUR

Terribly Tough Test Number Thirteen (from page 76)

1) **A big mistake**. 1 ♛xf7 gives Black a draw by stalemate. ☐ ☐
2) **No**. White is not stalemated – he still has the pawn move 1 f4. ☐ ☐
3) **1 ♛e8+** sets up a draw by *perpetual check* – 1...♚h7 2 ♛h5+ ♚g8 3 ♛e8+ etc. ☐ ☐
4) **1...♚c3** (the only move for Black to keep defending his pawn) **stalemates** the white king, so the game is drawn. ☐ ☐

Terribly Tough Test Number Fourteen (from page 82)

1) There are **three** ways to checkmate: 1...♛a1, 1...♛b1 and 1...♛d2. ☐ ☐
2) **1 ♛b2**. A mistake would be 1 ♚c5, putting Black in *stalemate*. ☐ ☐
3) **1 ♜b8** is checkmate. ☐ ☐
4) **1...♜g2+** forces White's king back (2 ♚c1 or 2 ♚b1 or 2 ♚a1) after which Black plays **2...♜h1 checkmate**. ☐ ☐

Now Add up Your Points for Part Four					
All 8	Grand Alligator Standard	6-7	Excellent!	4-5	Very Good
2-3	Average	0-1	More practice needed		

PART FIVE

Terribly Tough Test Number Fifteen (from page 88)

1) **1 ♘c7**. The knight *forks* the two black rooks. ☐ ☐
2) **1...♛d4+** *forks* the **white king on g1** and the **white rook on a1**. ☐ ☐
3) **1 ♗b5** *pins* the black queen against the black king. ☐ ☐
4) **1...♜a1+** is a *skewer*. White's king must move, when Black captures a rook for free with 2...♜xh1. ☐ ☐

Terribly Tough Test Number Sixteen (from page 96)

1) **1 e4** is a better opening move than 1 h3. It fights for central territory, and assists with White's later piece development. ☐ ☐
2) The **French Defense**. ☐ ☐
3) **No**, 3...♘f6 is **not** a good move: White has 4 ♛xf7 checkmate! ☐ ☐
4) **White** has a much better position: his piece development is more advanced, his pawns control the center, and he has already castled. ☐ ☐

Terribly Tough Test Number Seventeen (from page 100)

1) **1 ♛xd7!** wins: 1...♛xd7 2 ♜b8+ forces a back-rank checkmate next move. ☐ ☐
2) **1 ♜h8+!** (a rook sacrifice) ♚xh8 2 ♛h6+ ♚g8 3 ♛g7 checkmate. ☐ ☐
3) **1 ♜xh7** is crushing. On 1...♚xh7, 2 ♜h1+ ♚g8 3 ♜h8 is checkmate. ☐ ☐
4) The queen sacrifice **1 ♛g8+** forces either 1...♘xg8 or 1...♜xg8, whereupon 2 ♘f7 is checkmate. ☐ ☐

Now Add up Your Points for Part Five					
All 12	Grand Alligator Standard	8-11	Excellent!	6-7	Very Good
3-5	Average	0-2	More practice needed